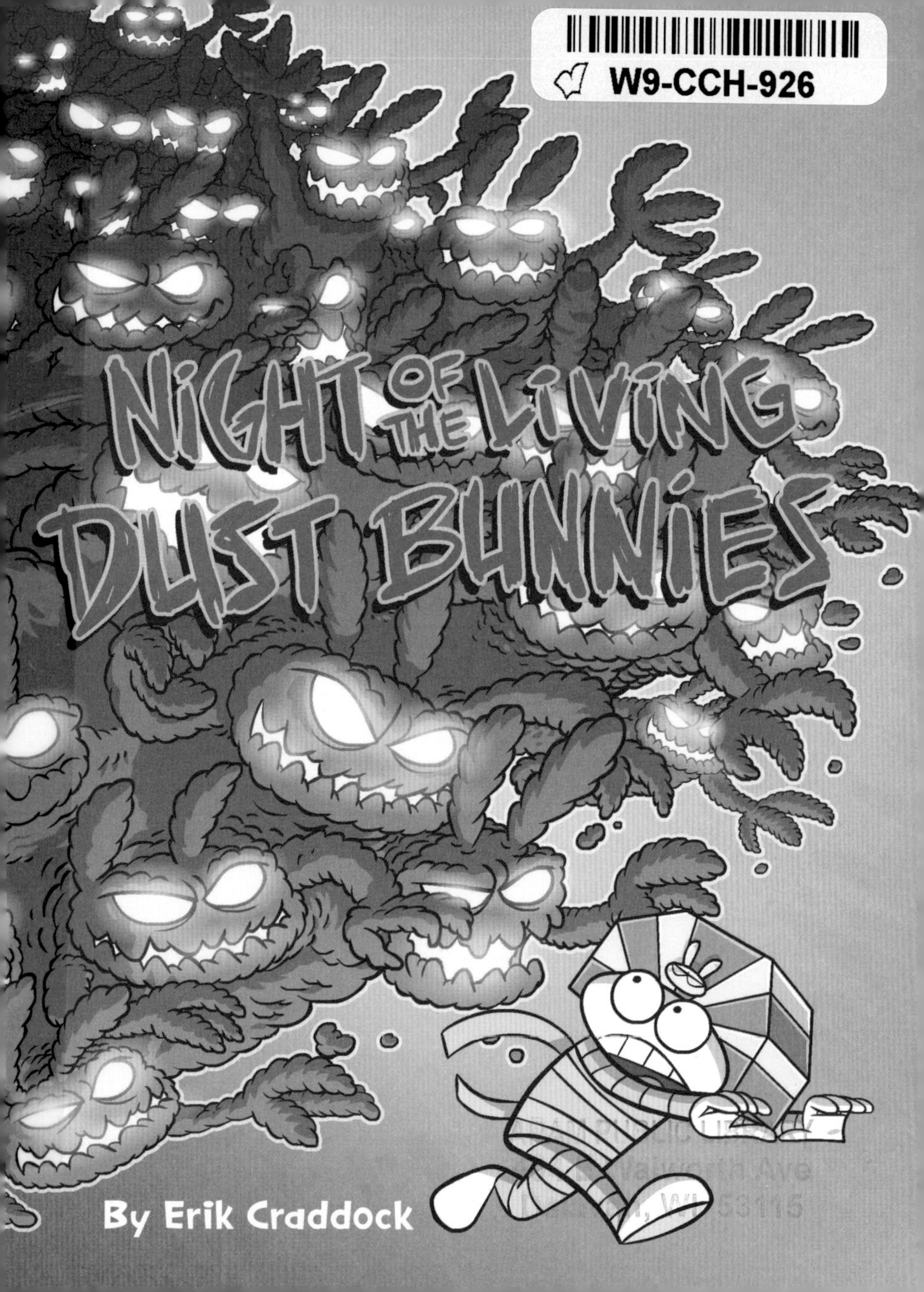
NIGHT OF THE LIVING DUST BUNNIES
By Erik Craddock

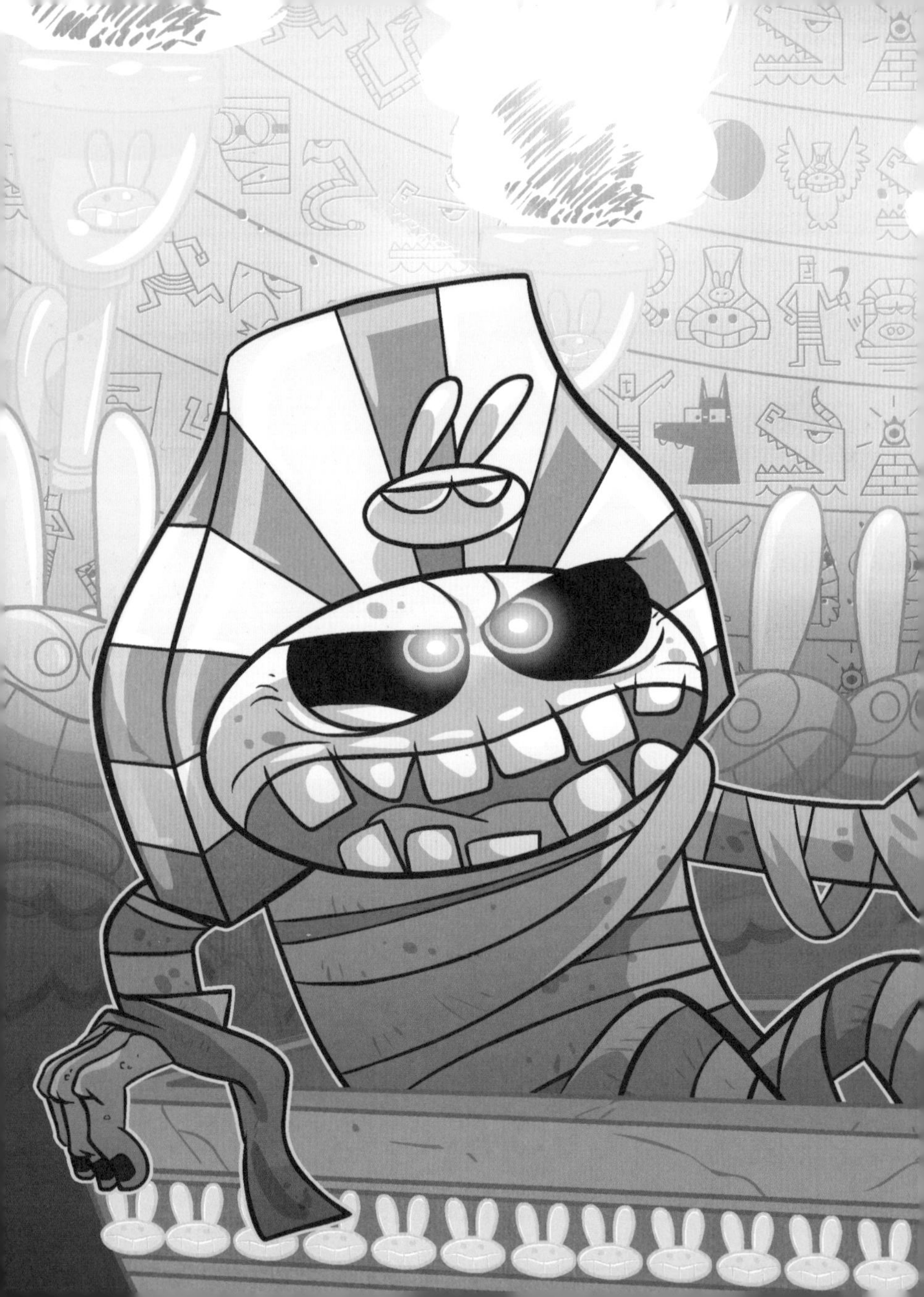

Visit us on the Web! www.randomhouse.com/kids

Educators and librarians, for a variety of teaching tools, visit us at www.randomhouse.com/teachers
stonerabbit.com

Library of Congress Cataloging-in-Publication Data
Craddock, Erik.
Night of the living dust bunnies / by Erik Craddock.
p. cm.
Summary: While Stone Rabbit, Andy Wolf, and Henri Tortoise are trick-or-treating, zombie dust bunnies are taking over their town.
ISBN 978-0-375-86724-8 (pbk.) — ISBN 978-0-375-96724-5 (lib. bdg.)
1. Graphic novels. [1. Graphic novels. 2. Halloween—Fiction. 3. Zombies—Fiction. 4. Dust—Fiction. 5. Rabbits—Fiction. 6. Animals—Fiction. 7. Humorous stories.] I. Title.
PZ7.7.C73Nh 2011 [Fic]—dc22 2010023489

MANUFACTURED IN MALAYSIA 10 9 8 7 6 5 4 First Edition

Random House Children's Books supports the First Amendment and celebrates the right to read.

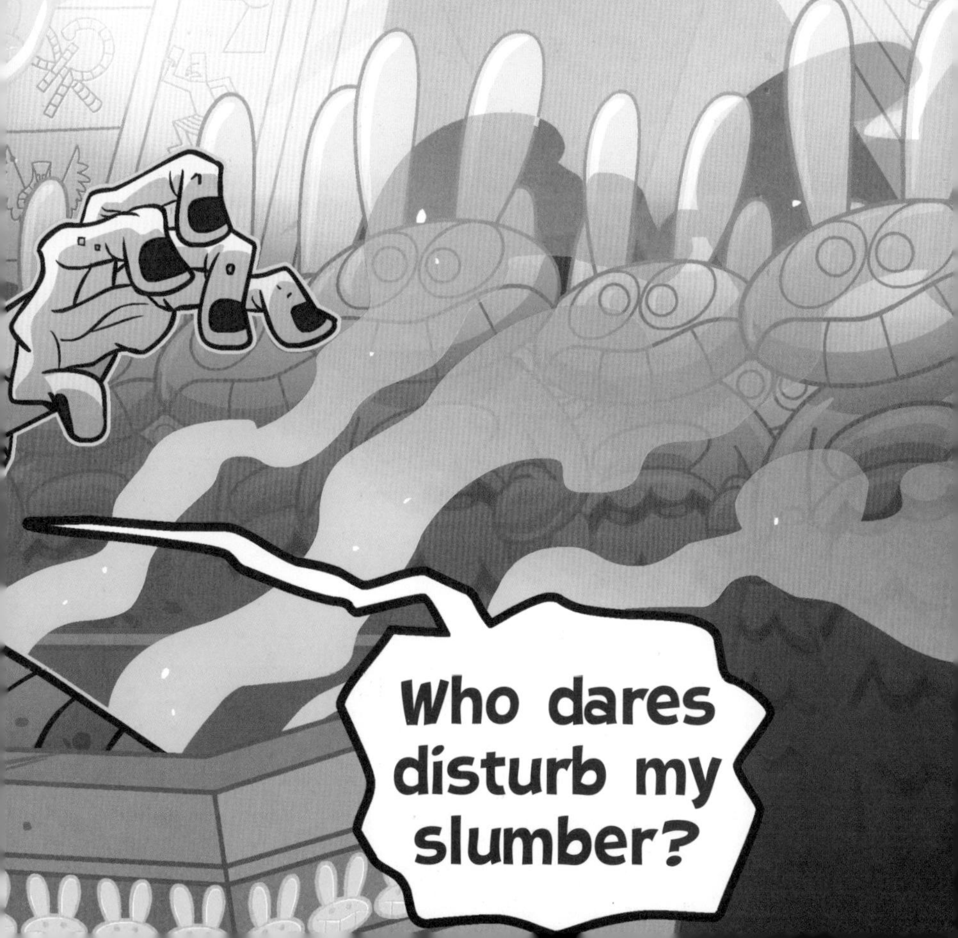
Who dares disturb my slumber?

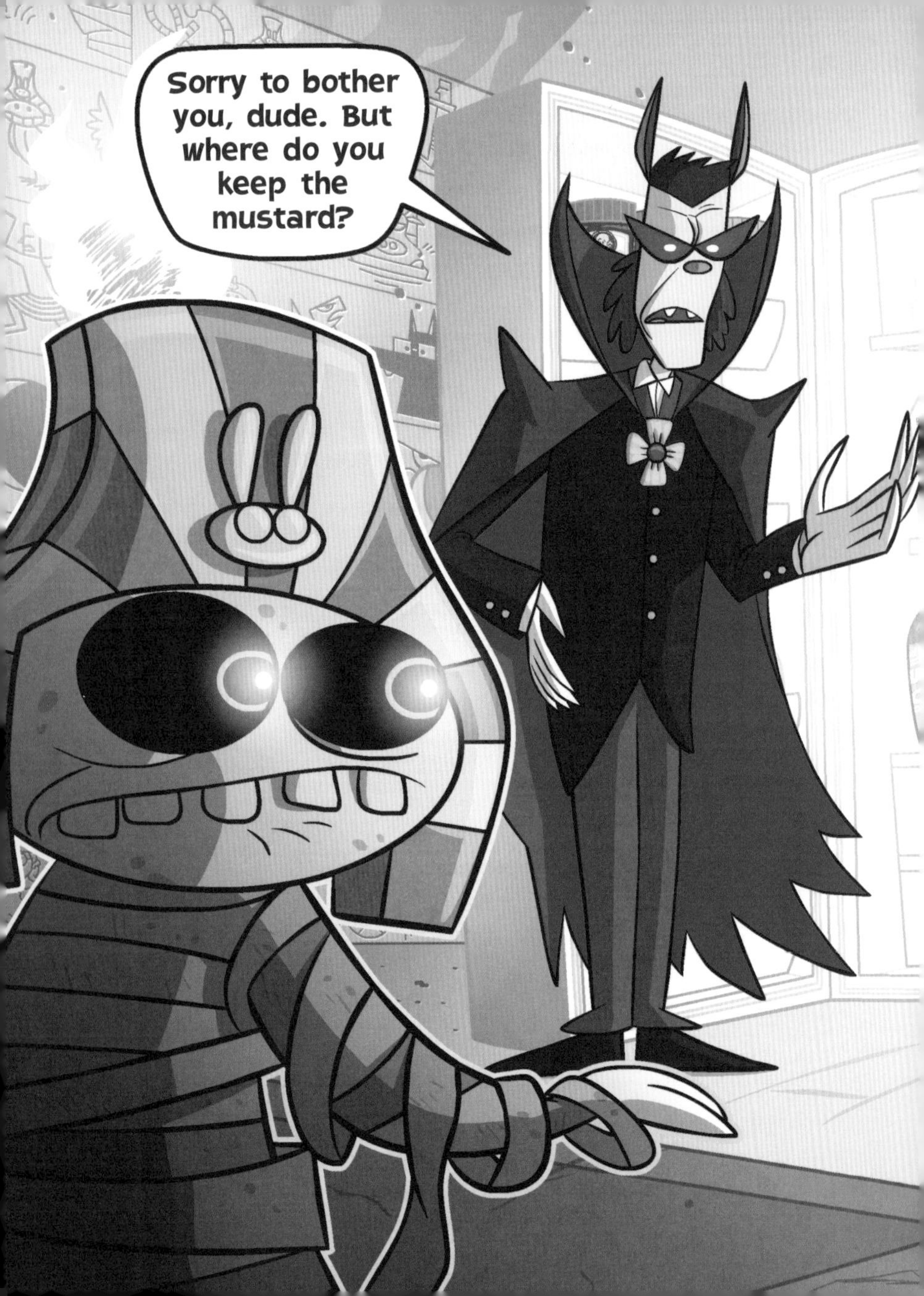
Sorry to bother you, dude. But where do you keep the mustard?

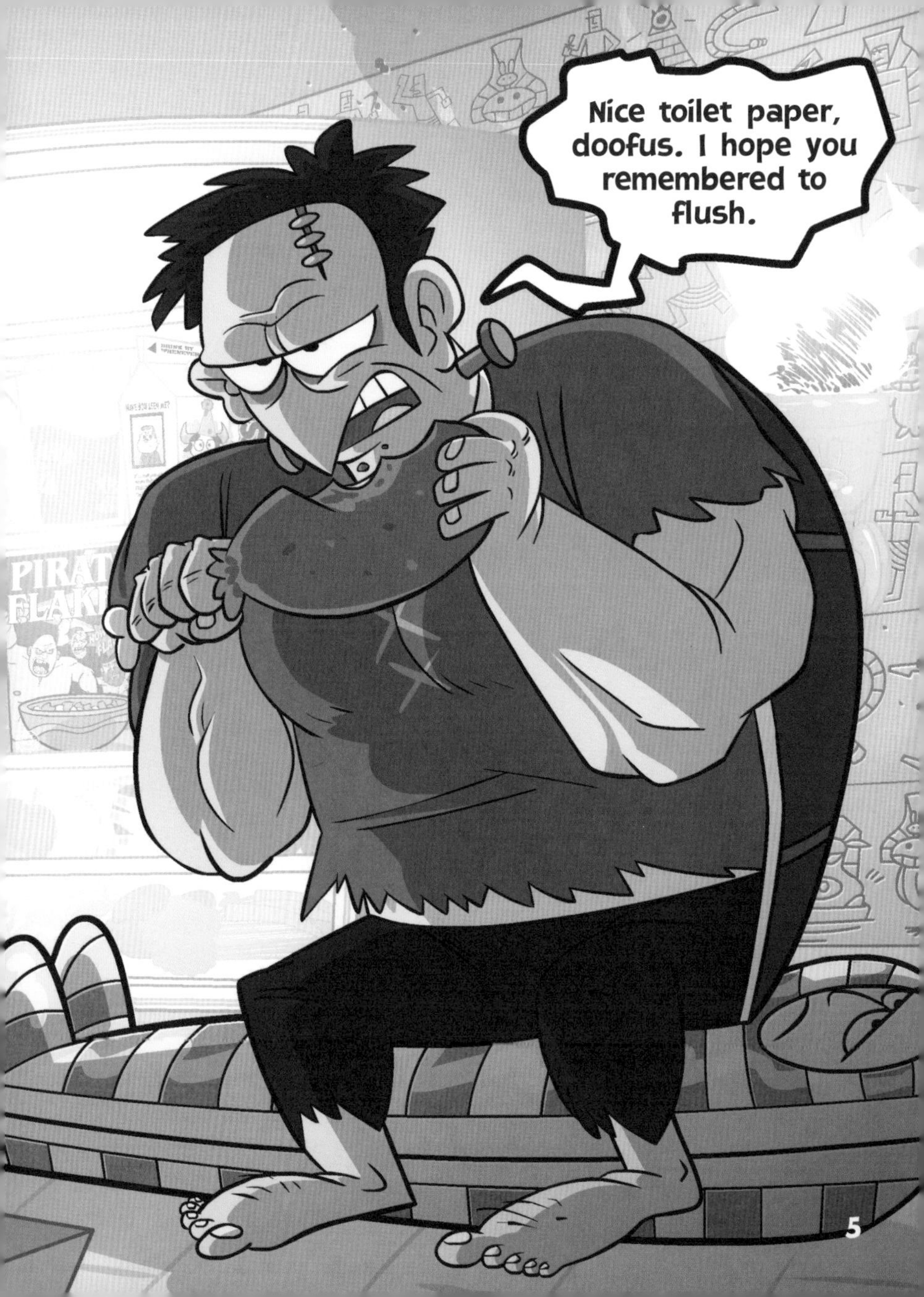
Nice toilet paper, doofus. I hope you remembered to flush.

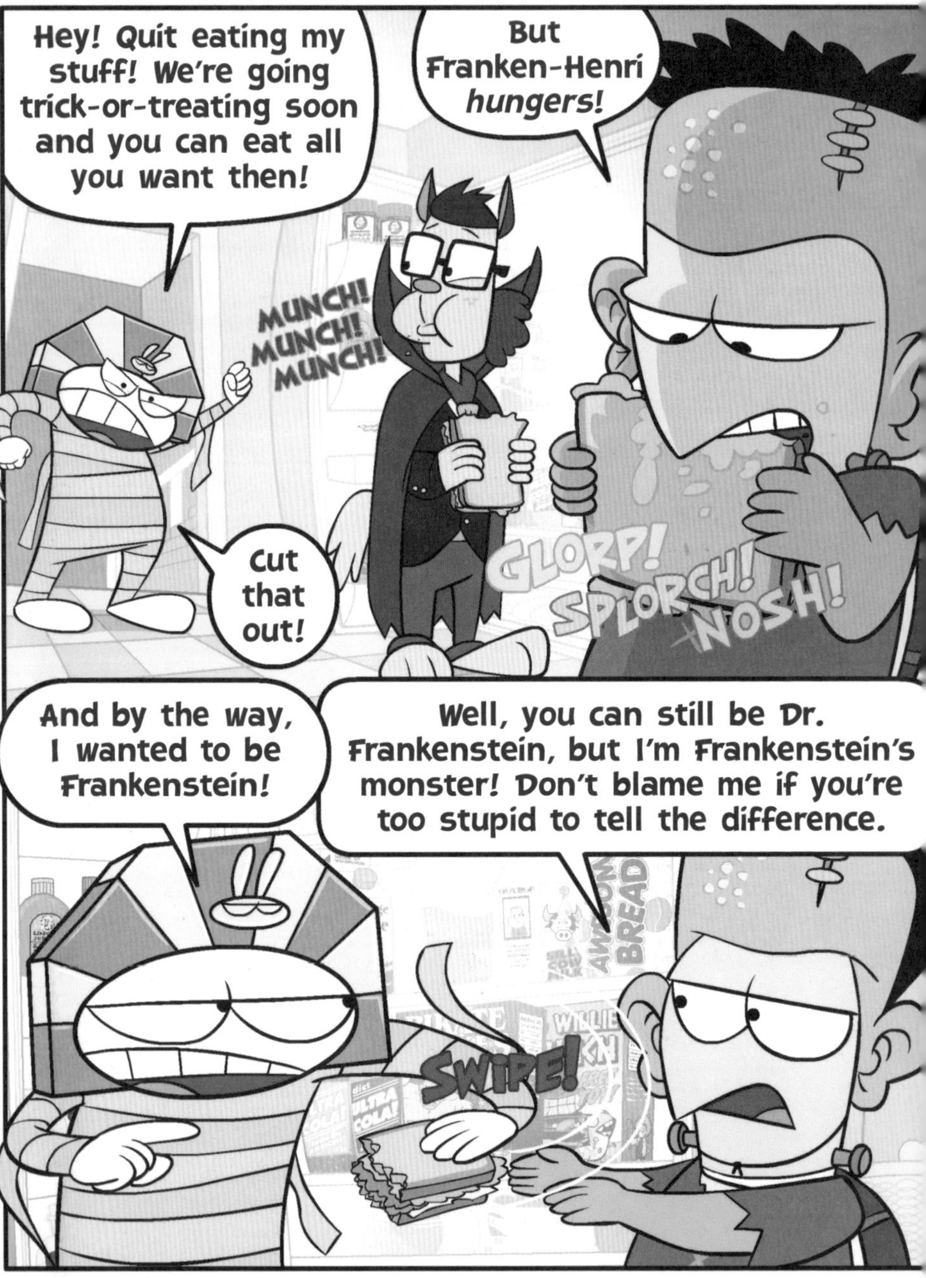
Hey! Quit eating my stuff! We're going trick-or-treating soon and you can eat all you want then!
But Franken-Henri *hungers!*
MUNCH! MUNCH! MUNCH!
GLORP! SPLORCH! NOSH!
Cut that out!
And by the way, I wanted to be Frankenstein!
Well, you can still be Dr. Frankenstein, but I'm Frankenstein's monster! Don't blame me if you're too stupid to tell the difference.
BREAD
ULTRA COLA!
SWIPE!

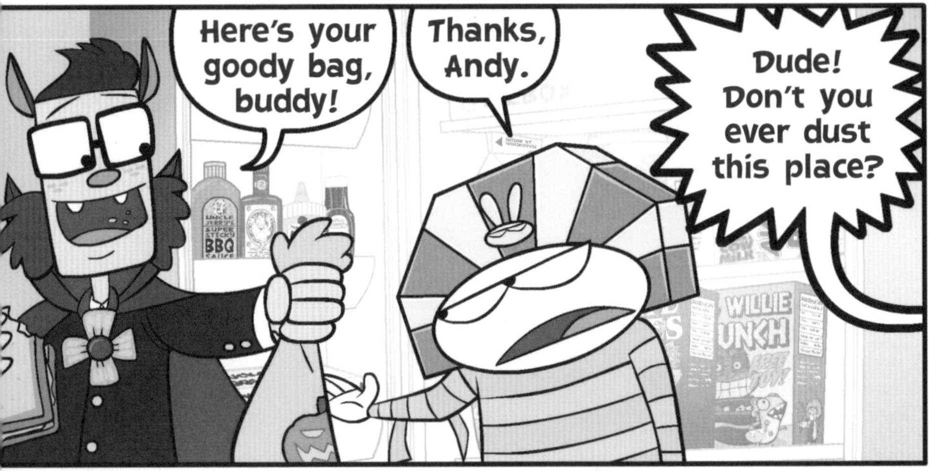
Here's your goody bag, buddy!
Thanks, Andy.
Dude! Don't you ever dust this place?

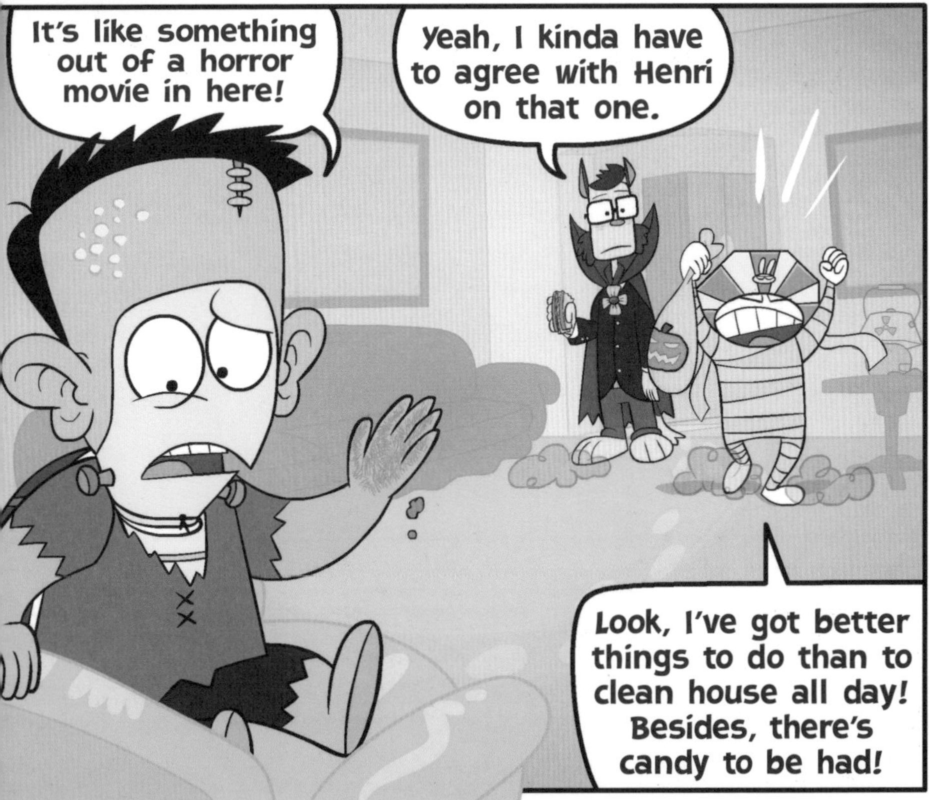
It's like something out of a horror movie in here!
Yeah, I kinda have to agree with Henri on that one.
Look, I've got better things to do than to clean house all day! Besides, there's candy to be had!

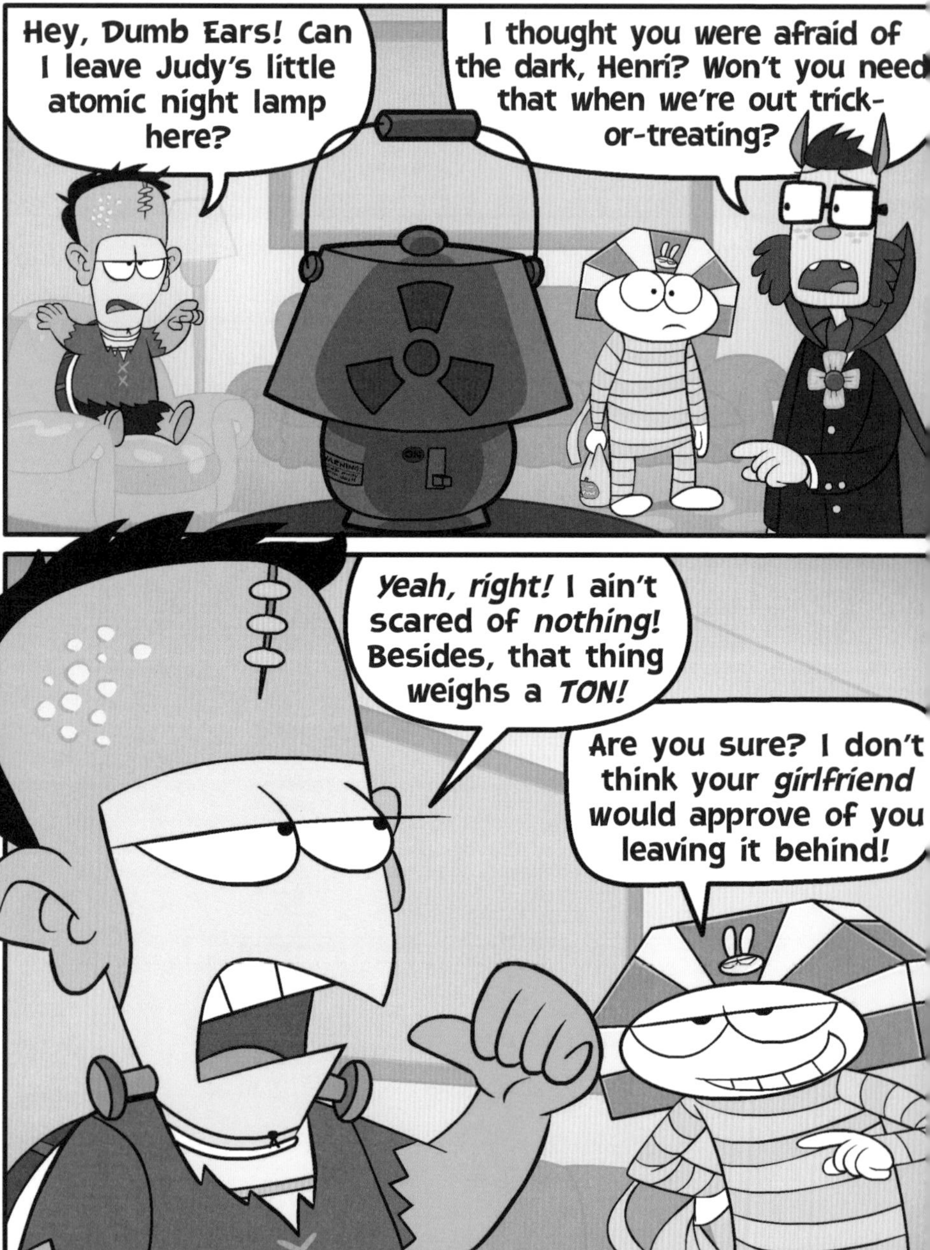
Hey, Dumb Ears! Can I leave Judy's little atomic night lamp here?
I thought you were afraid of the dark, Henri? Won't you need that when we're out trick-or-treating?
Yeah, right! I ain't scared of nothing! Besides, that thing weighs a TON!
Are you sure? I don't think your girlfriend would approve of you leaving it behind!

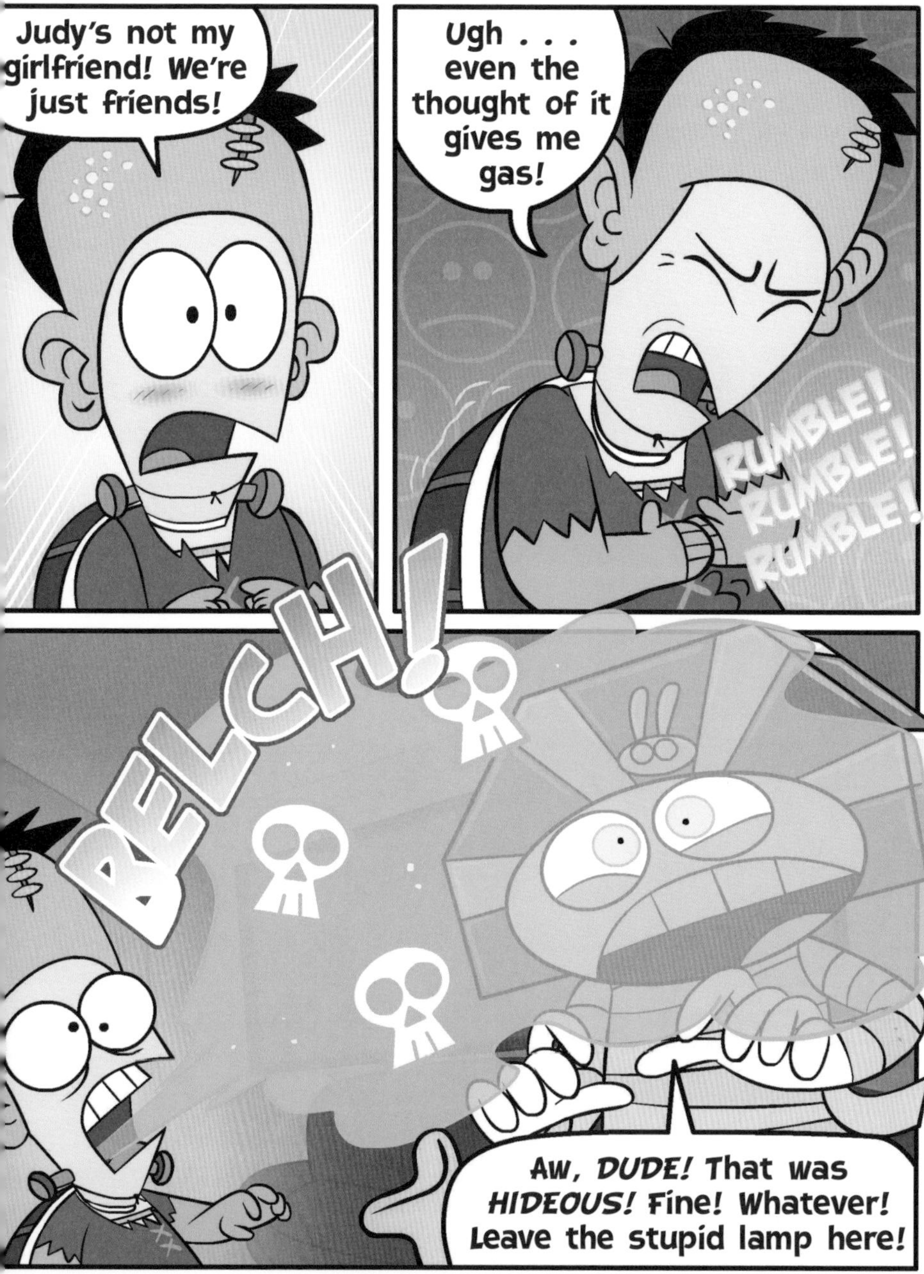
Judy's not my girlfriend! We're just friends!
Ugh . . . even the thought of it gives me gas!
RUMBLE! RUMBLE! RUMBLE!
BELCH!
Aw, DUDE! That was HIDEOUS! Fine! Whatever! Leave the stupid lamp here!

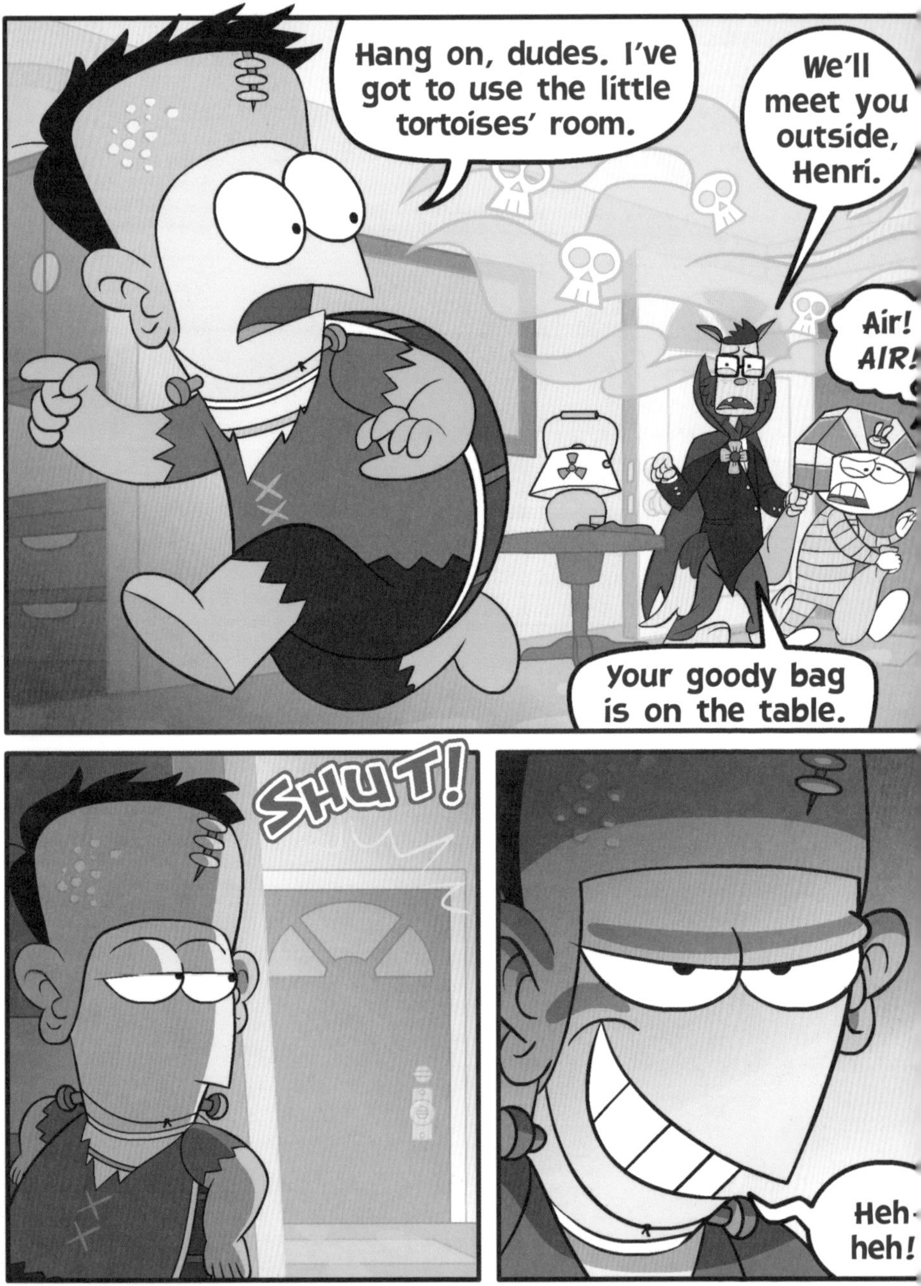
Hang on, dudes. I've got to use the little tortoises' room.
We'll meet you outside, Henri.
Air! AIR!
Your goody bag is on the table.
SHUT!
Heh-heh!

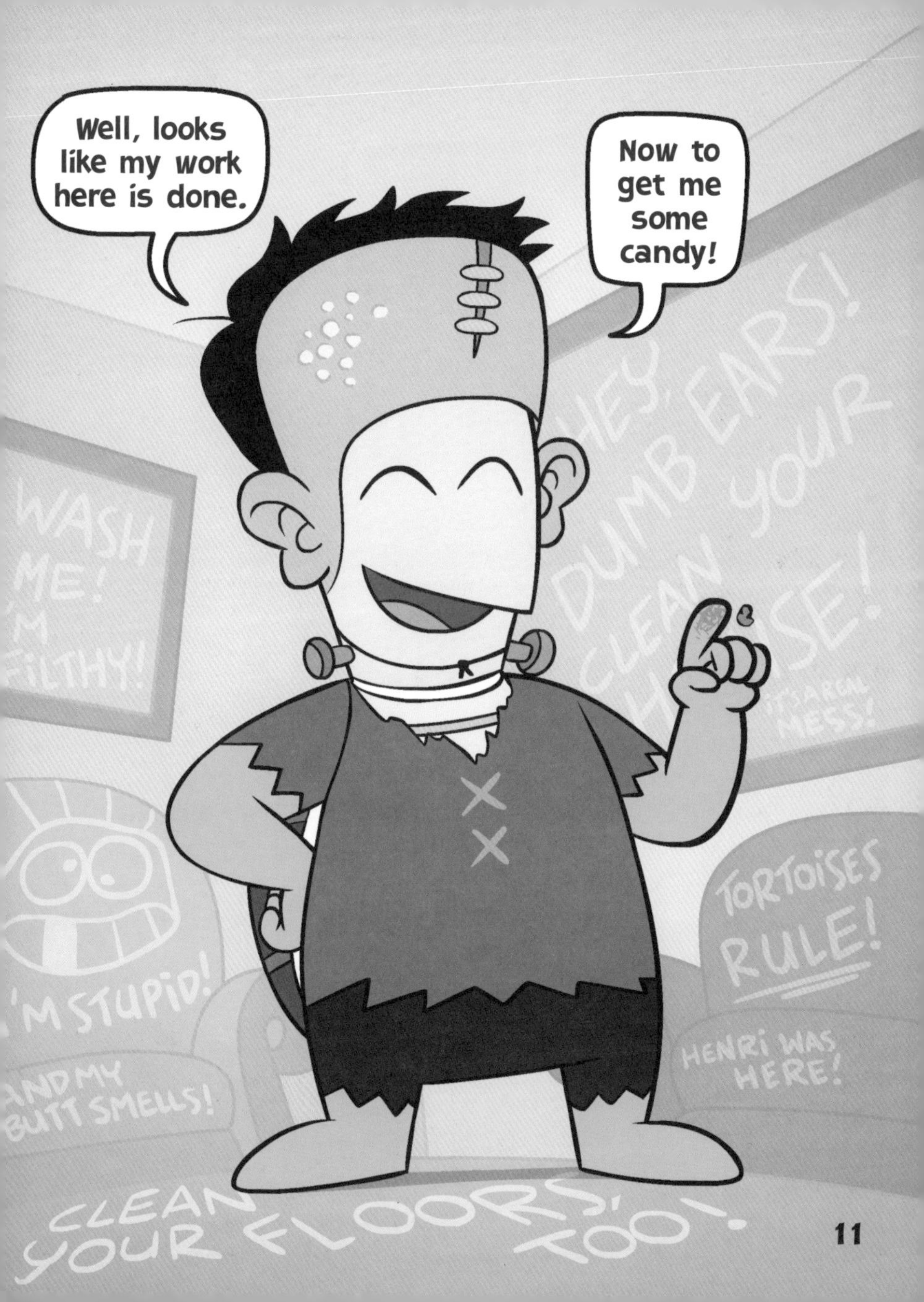
Well, looks like my work here is done.
Now to get me some candy!
WASH ME! 'M FILTHY!
HEY, DUMB EARS! CLEAN YOUR
IT'S A REAL MESS!
'M STUPID!
AND MY BUTT SMELLS!
TORTOISES RULE!
HENRI WAS HERE!
CLEAN YOUR FLOORS, TOO!

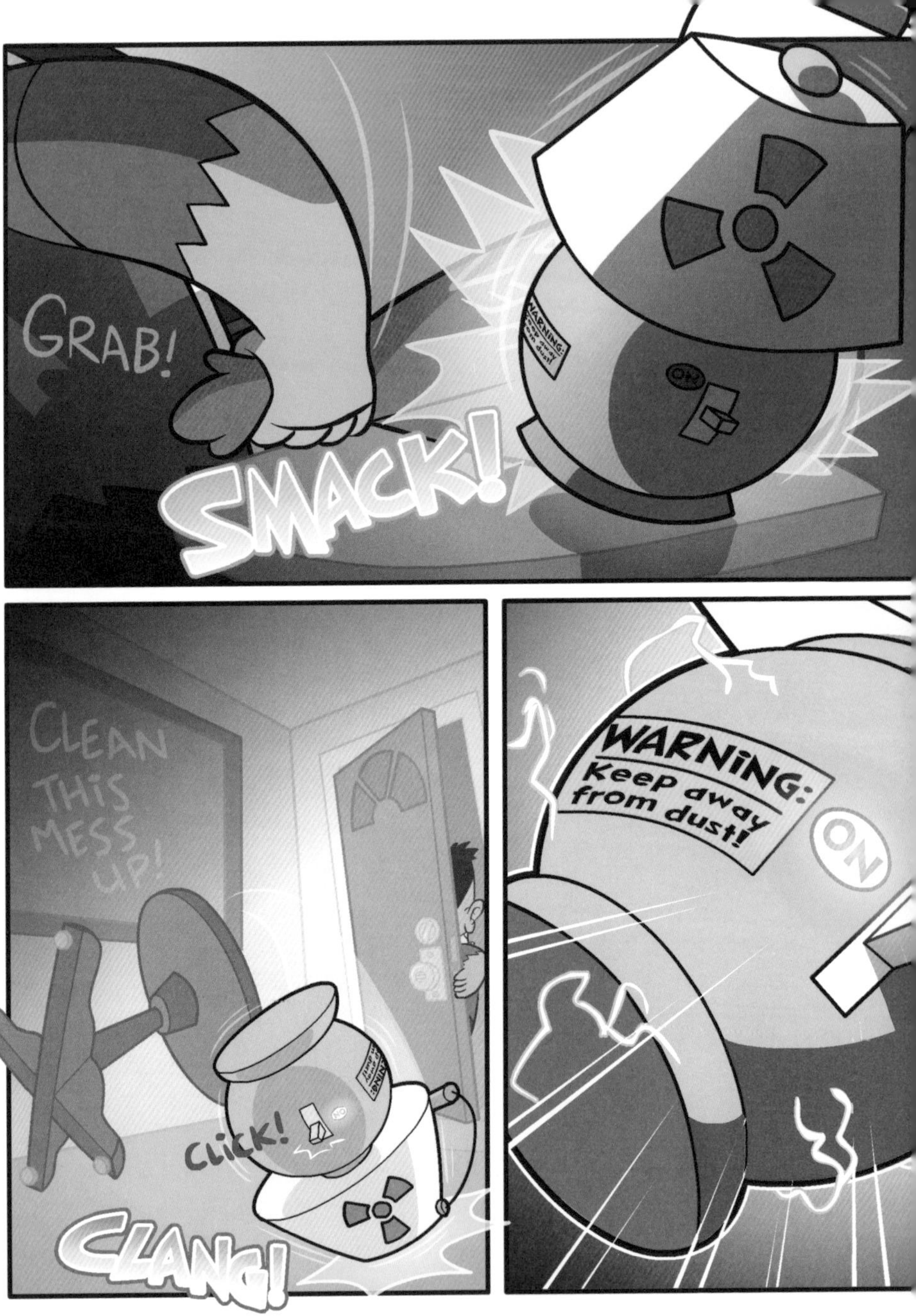
GRAB!
WARNING: Keep away from dust!
ON
SMACK!
CLEAN THIS MESS UP!
CLICK!
ON
CLANG!
WARNING: Keep away from dust!
ON

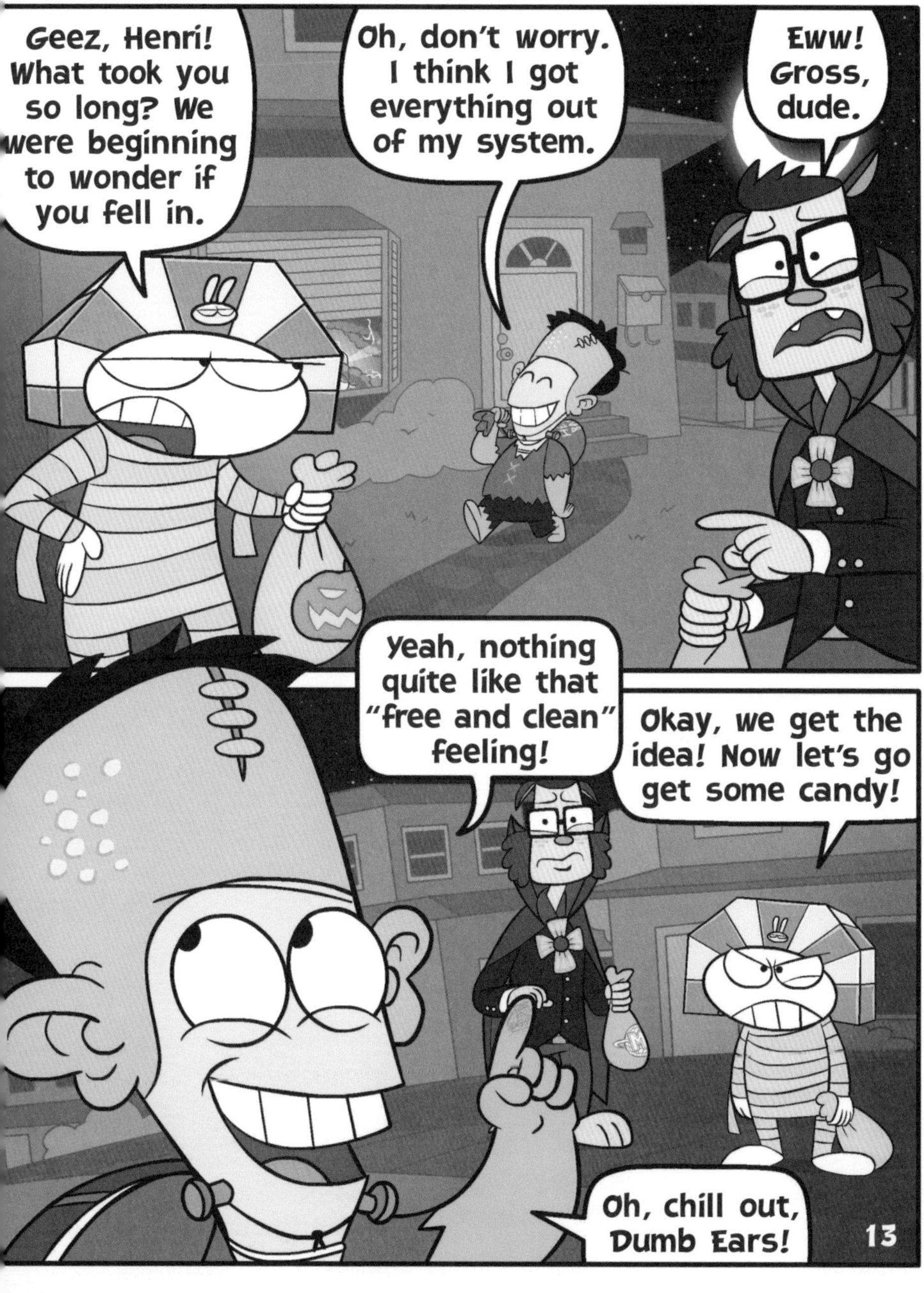
Geez, Henri! What took you so long? We were beginning to wonder if you fell in.
Oh, don't worry. I think I got everything out of my system.
Eww! Gross, dude.
Yeah, nothing quite like that "free and clean" feeling!
Okay, we get the idea! Now let's go get some candy!
Oh, chill out, Dumb Ears!

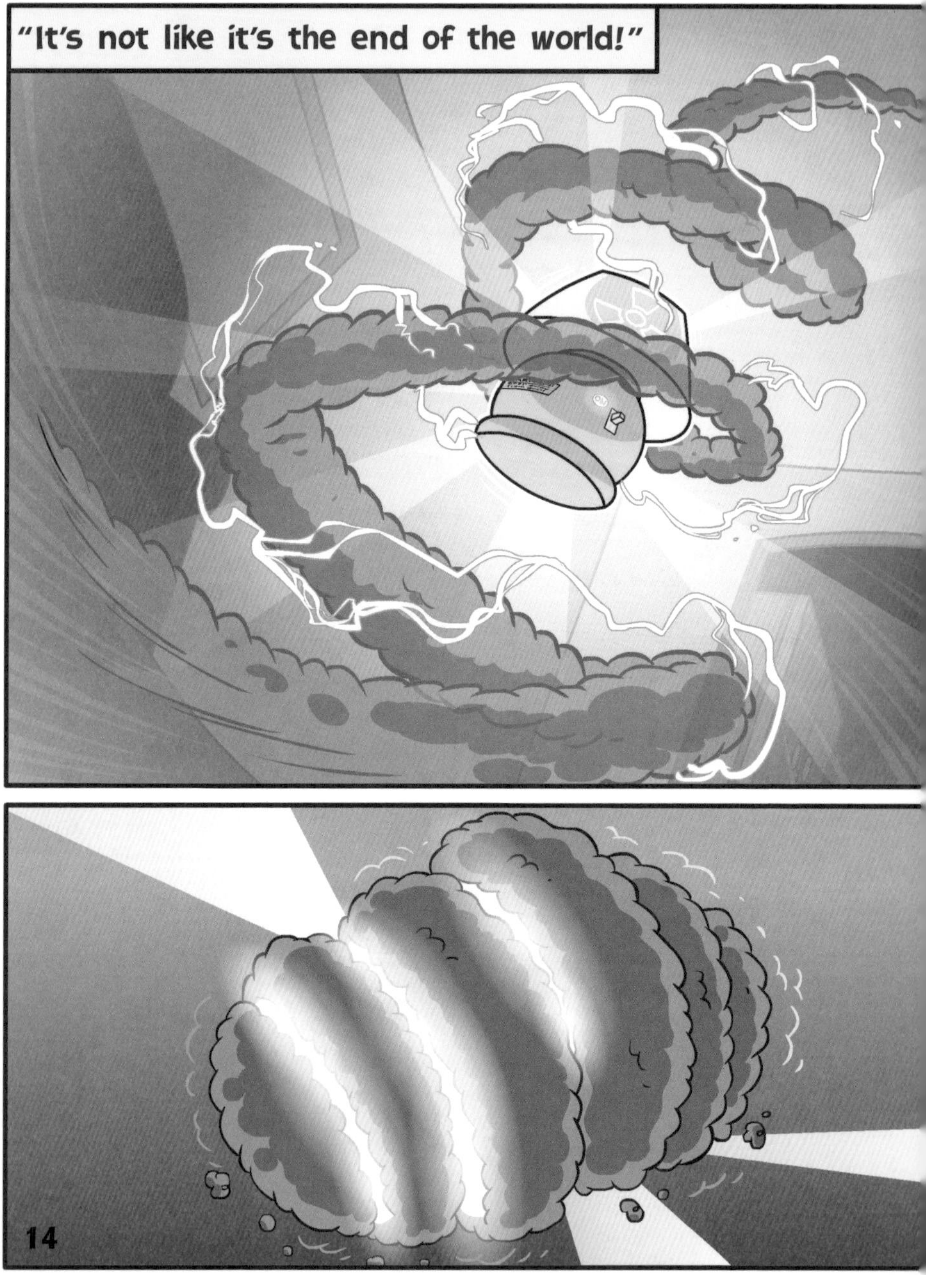
"It's not like it's the end of the world!"

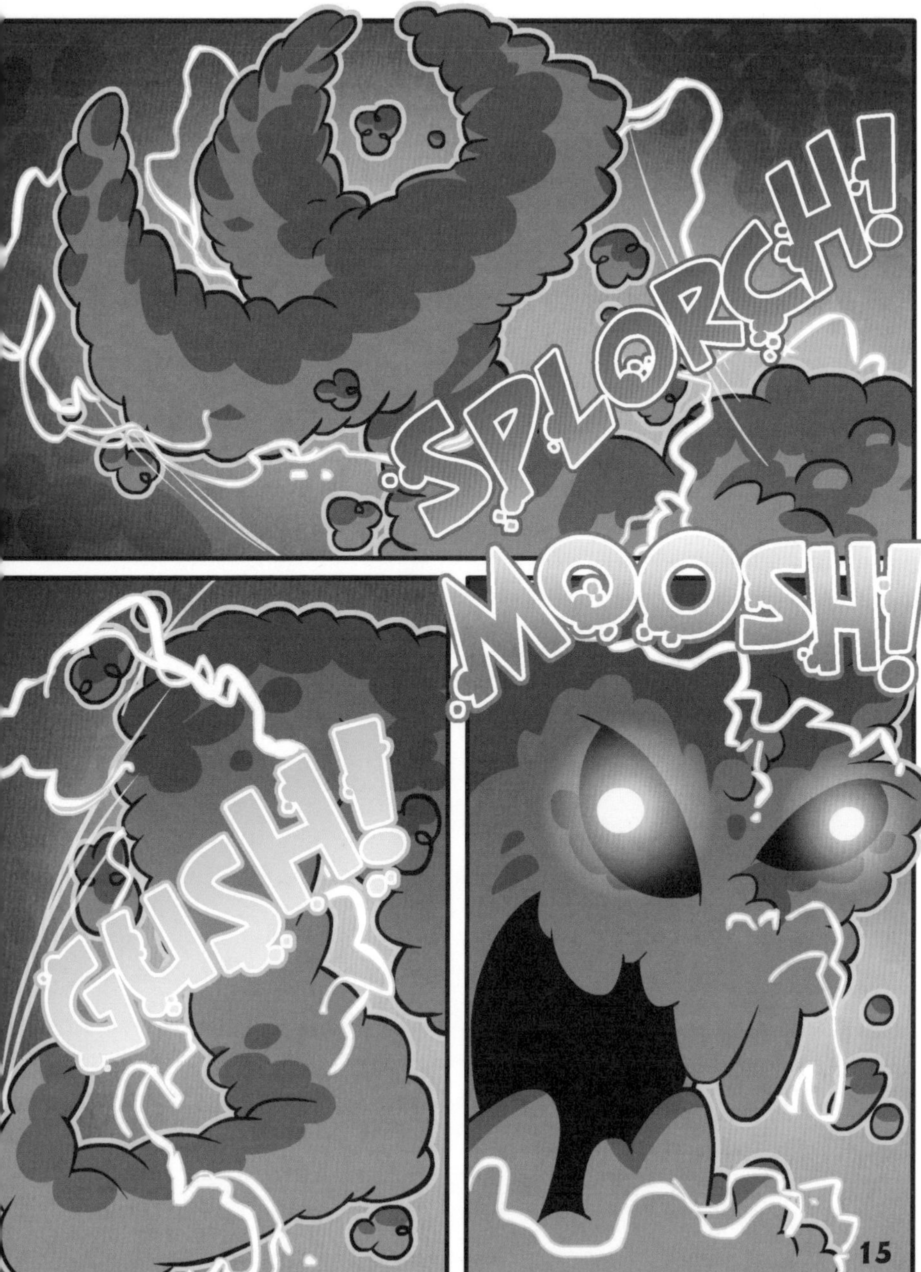
SPLORCH!
MOOSH!
GUSH!

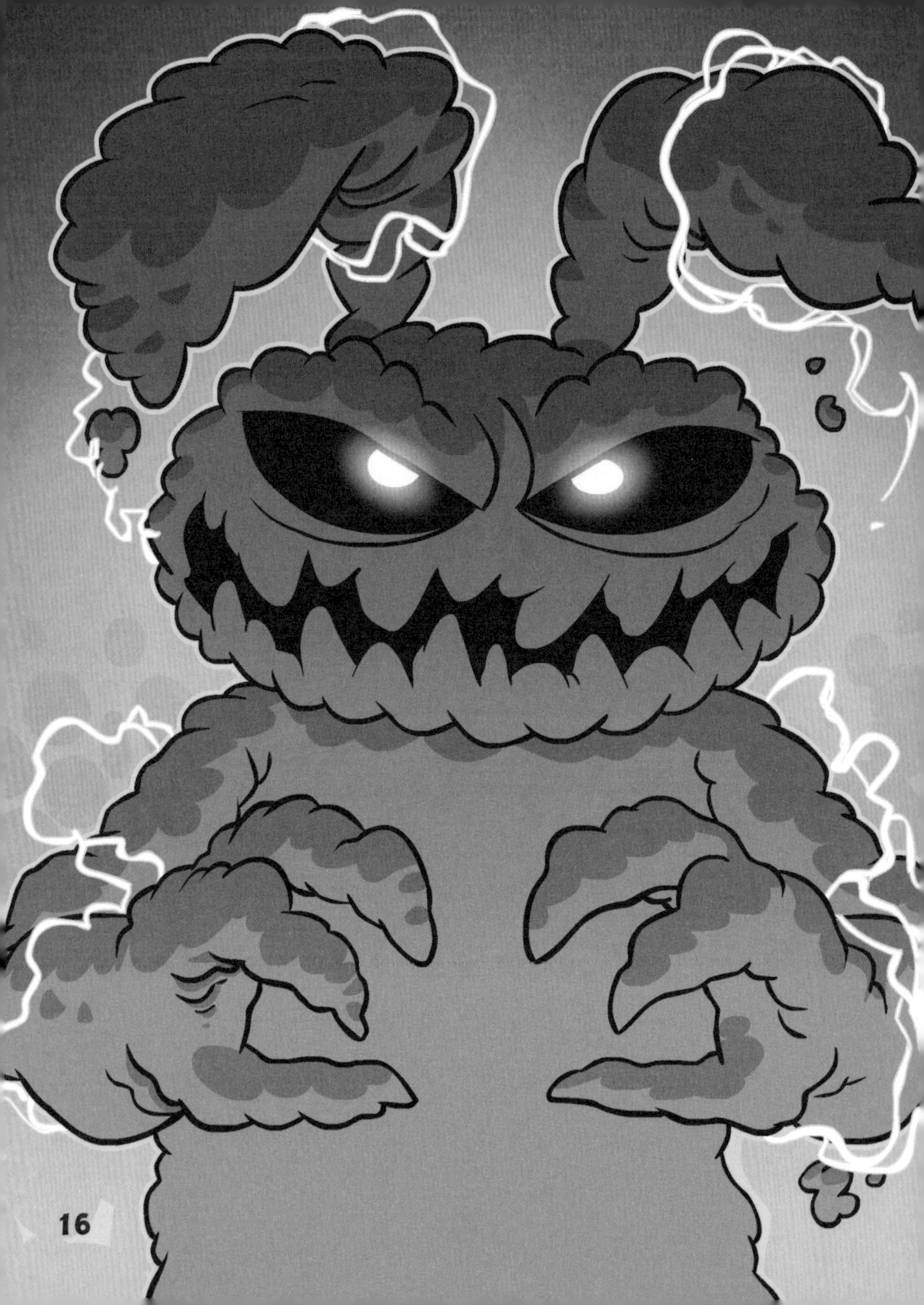

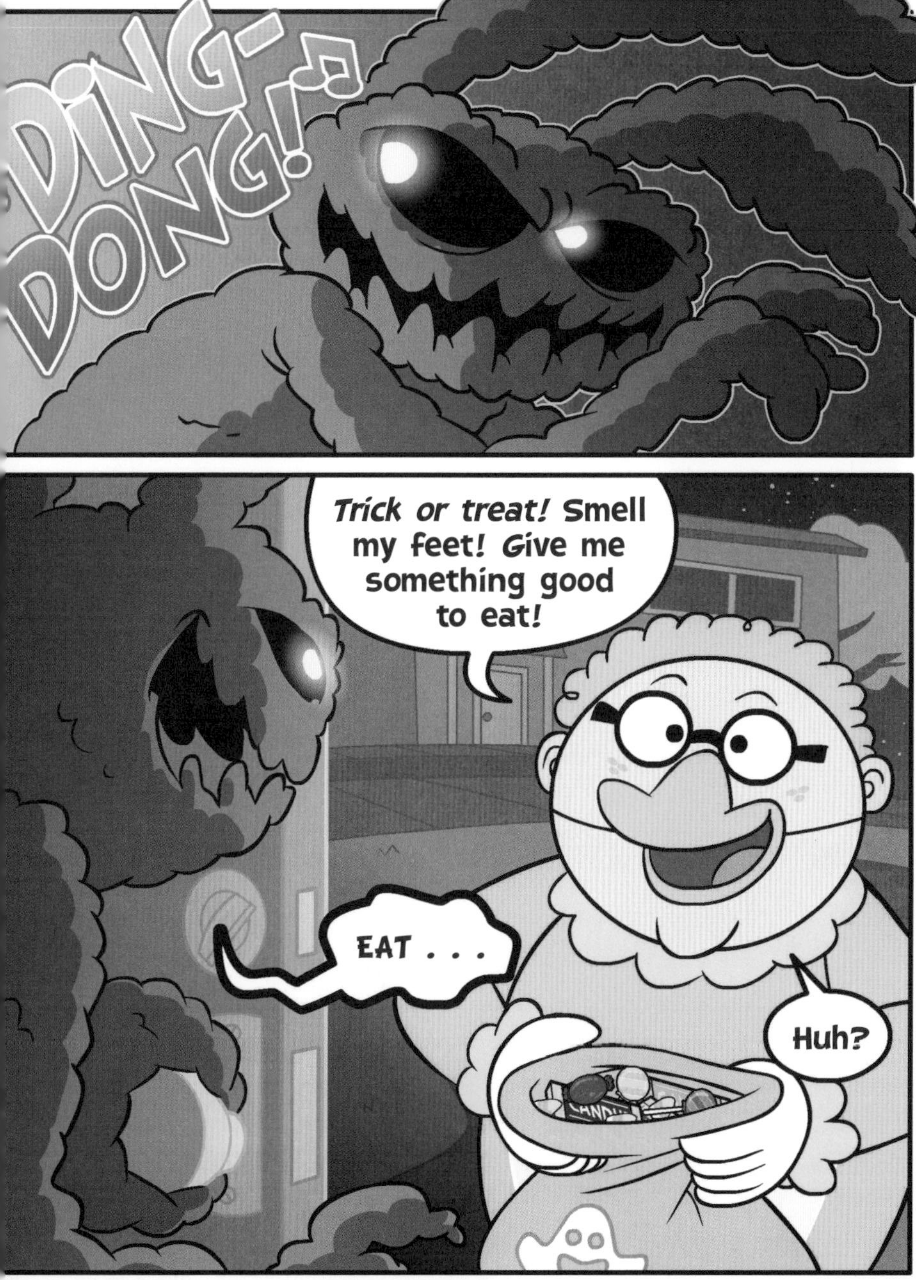
DING-DONG!
Trick or treat! Smell my feet! Give me something good to eat!
EAT . . .
Huh?

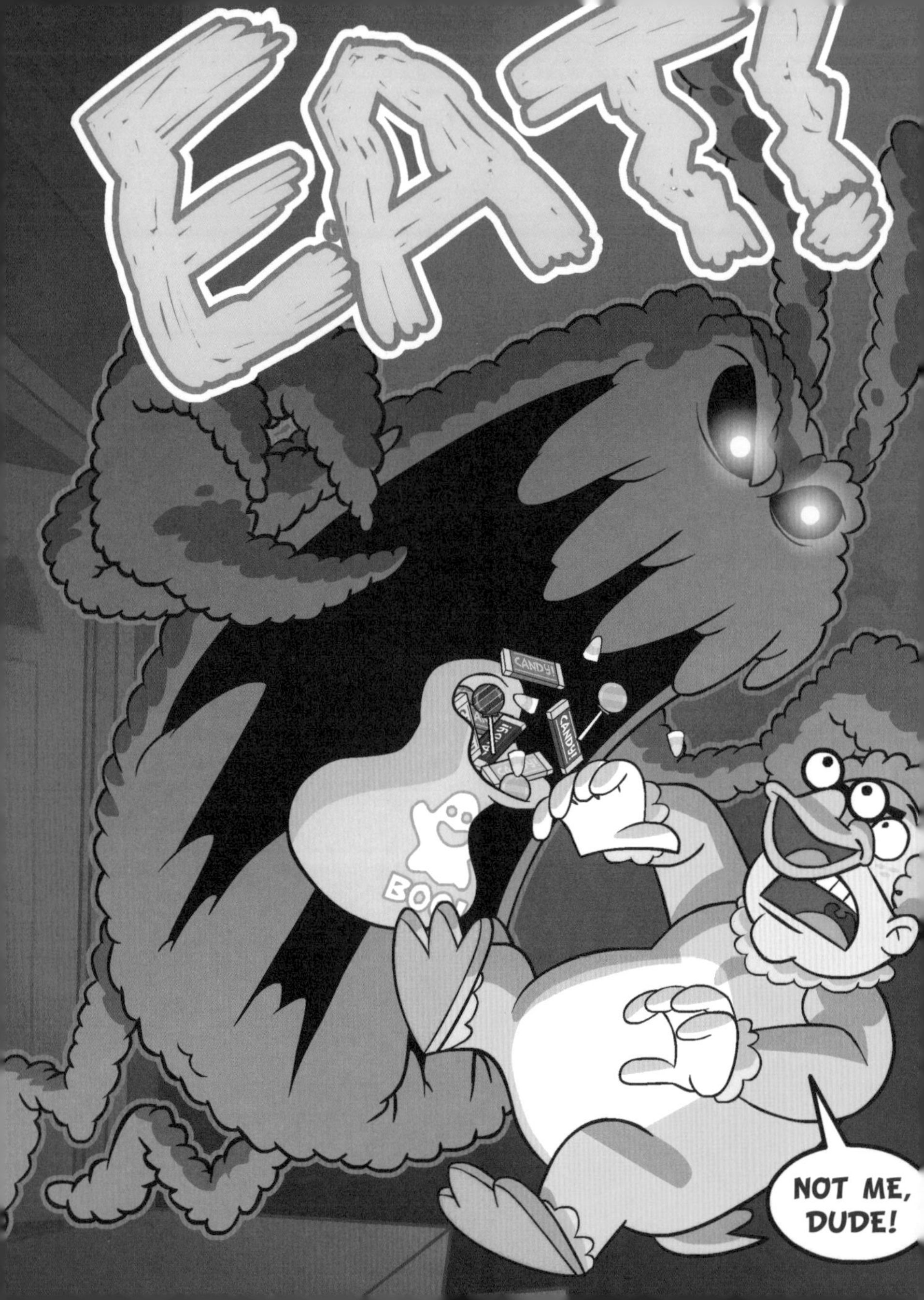
EAT!
CANDY!
CANDY!
BOO
NOT ME, DUDE!

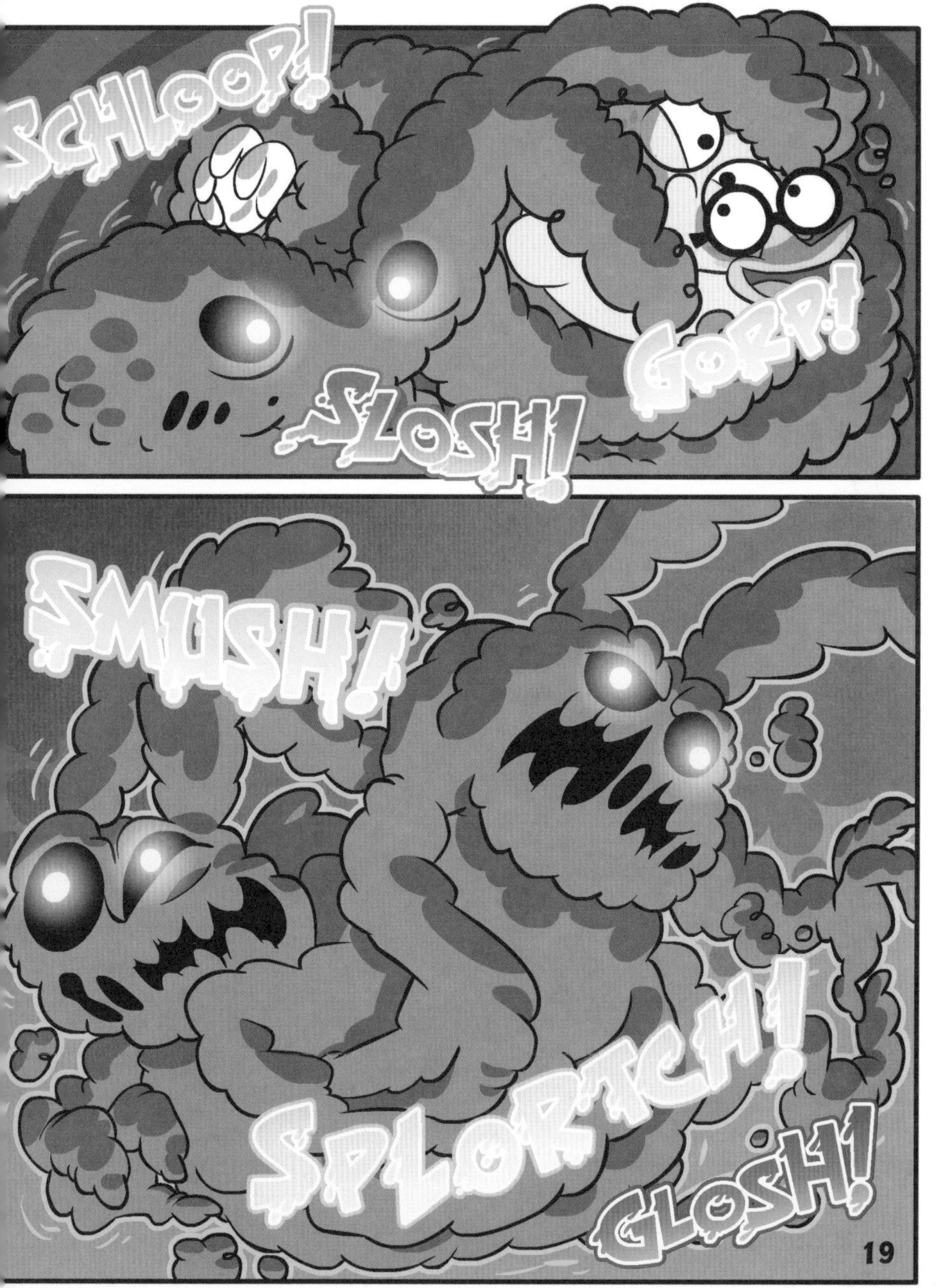
SCHLOOP!
SLOSH!
GORP!
SMUSH!
SPLORTCH!
GLOSH!

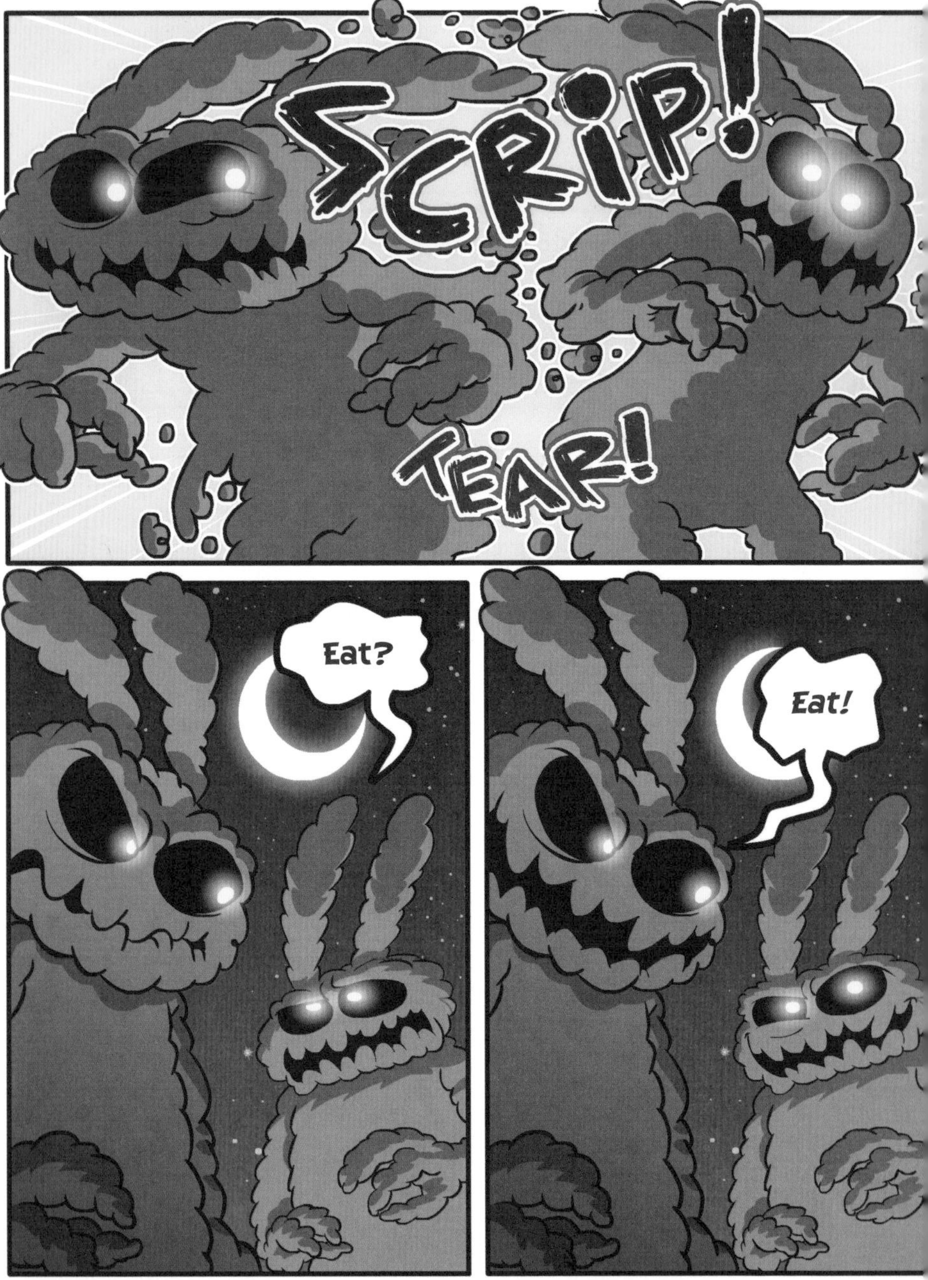
SCRIP!
TEAR!
Eat?
Eat!

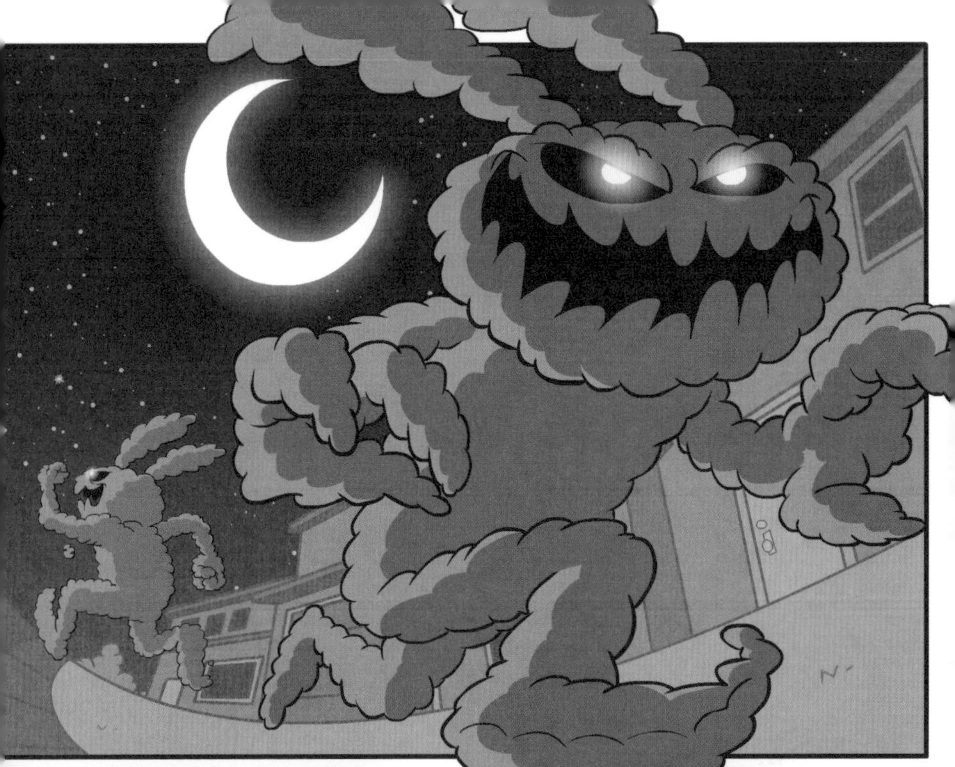

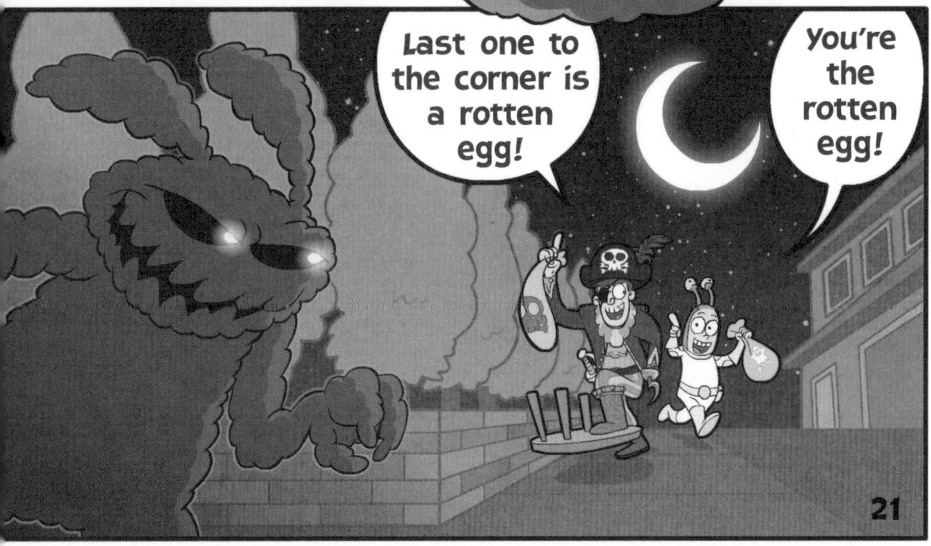
Last one to the corner is a rotten egg!
You're the rotten egg!

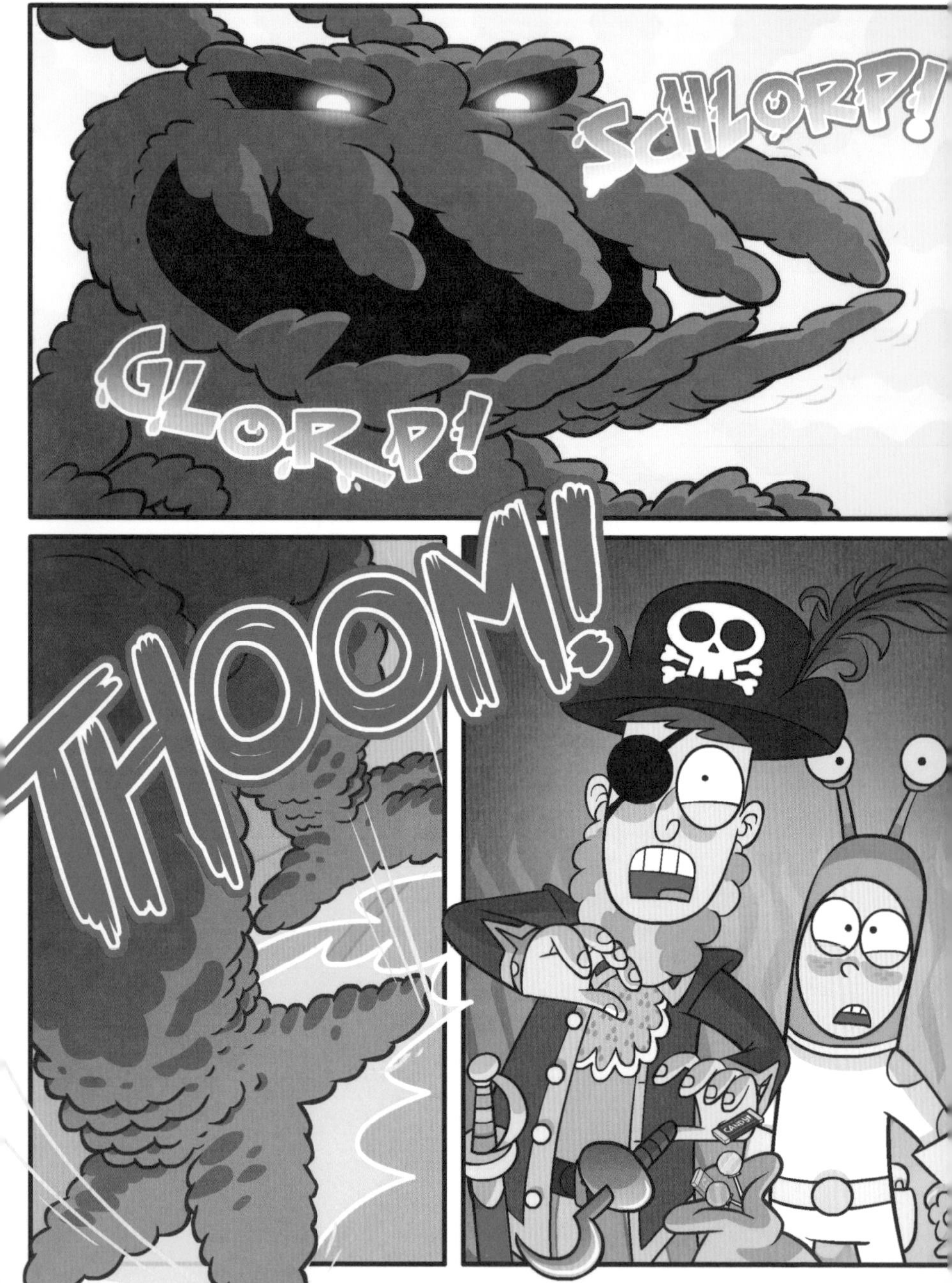
SCHLORP!
GLORP!
THOOM!
CANDY

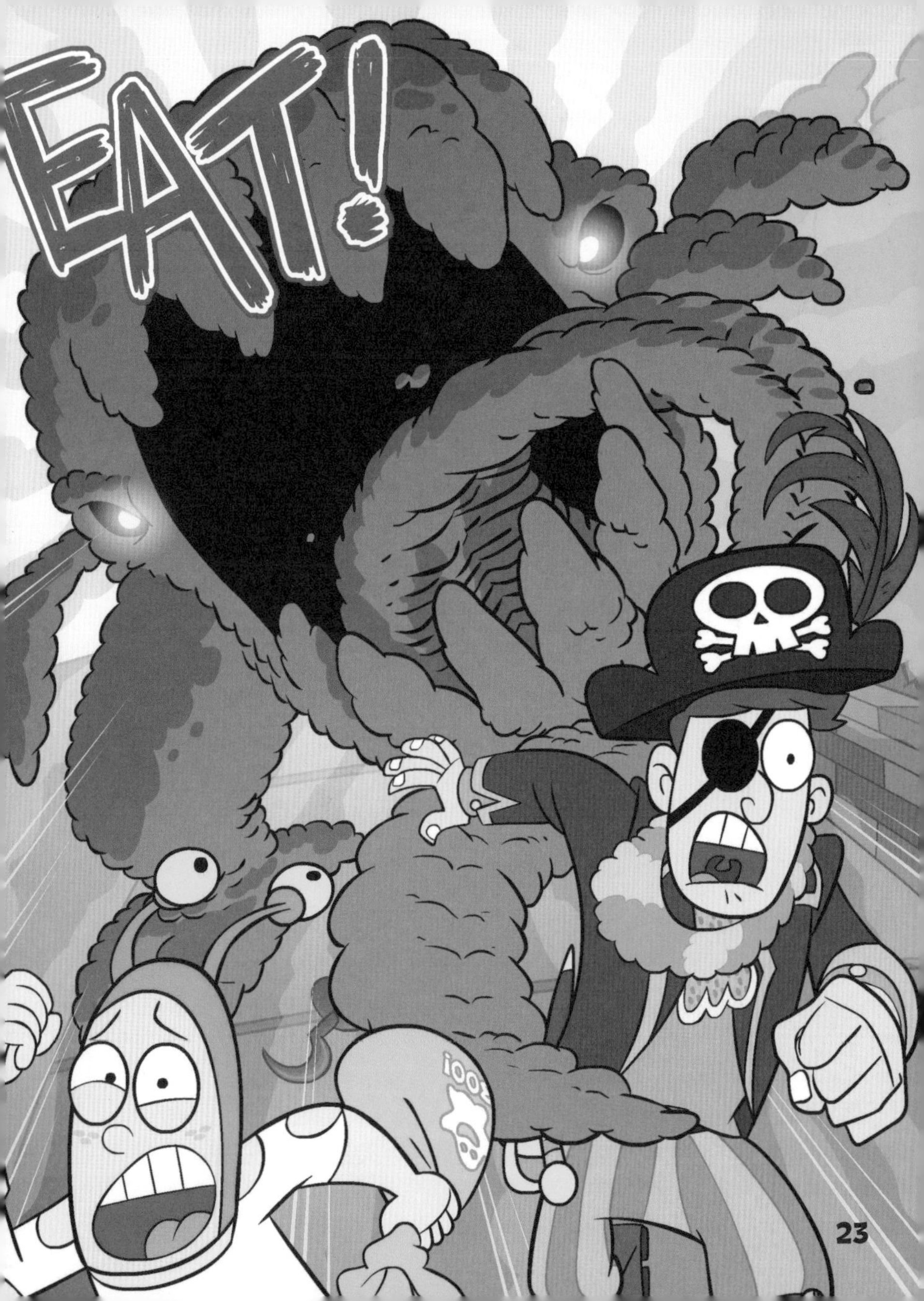
EAT!

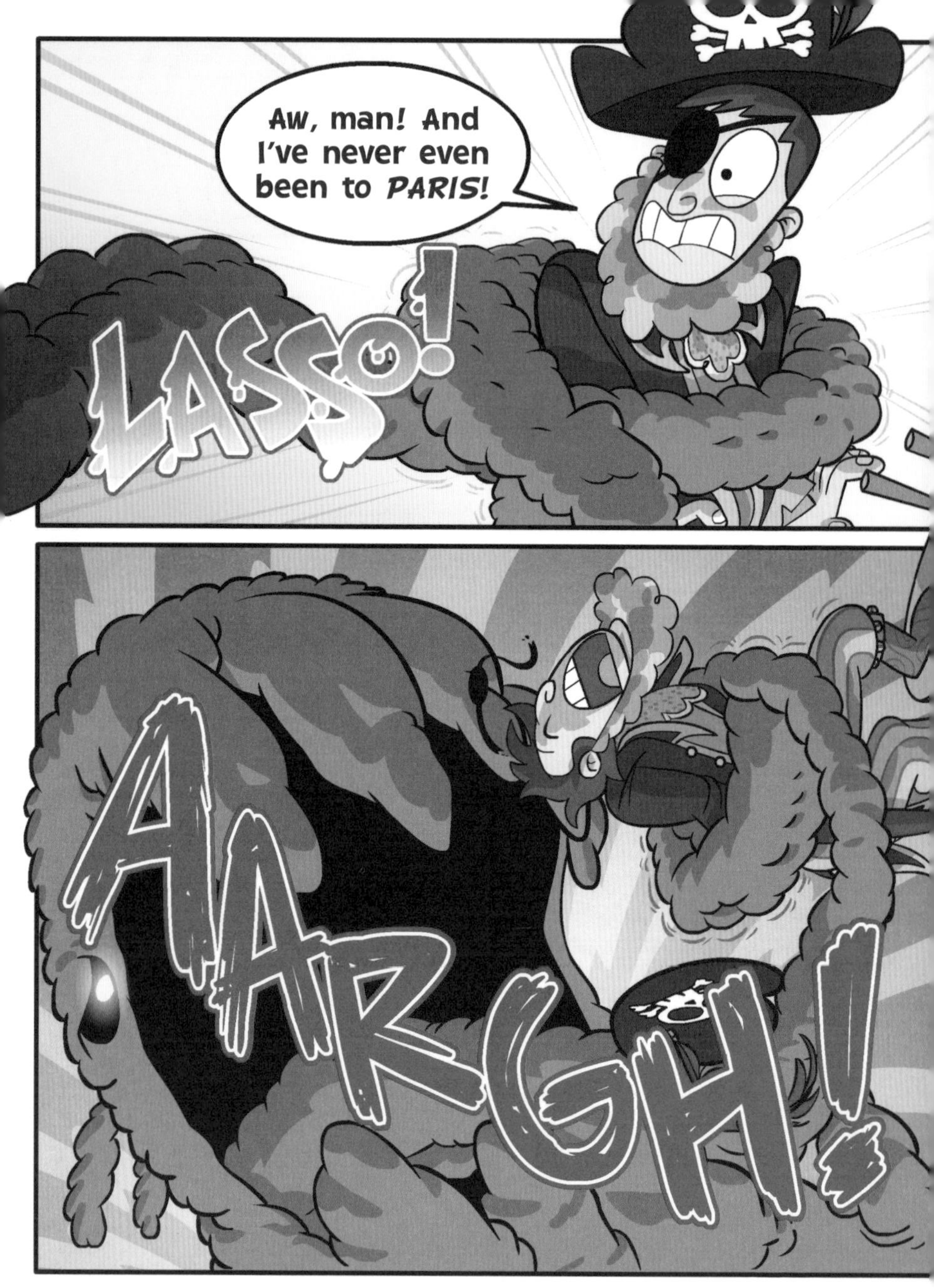
Aw, man! And I've never even been to *PARIS*!
LASSO!
AARGH!

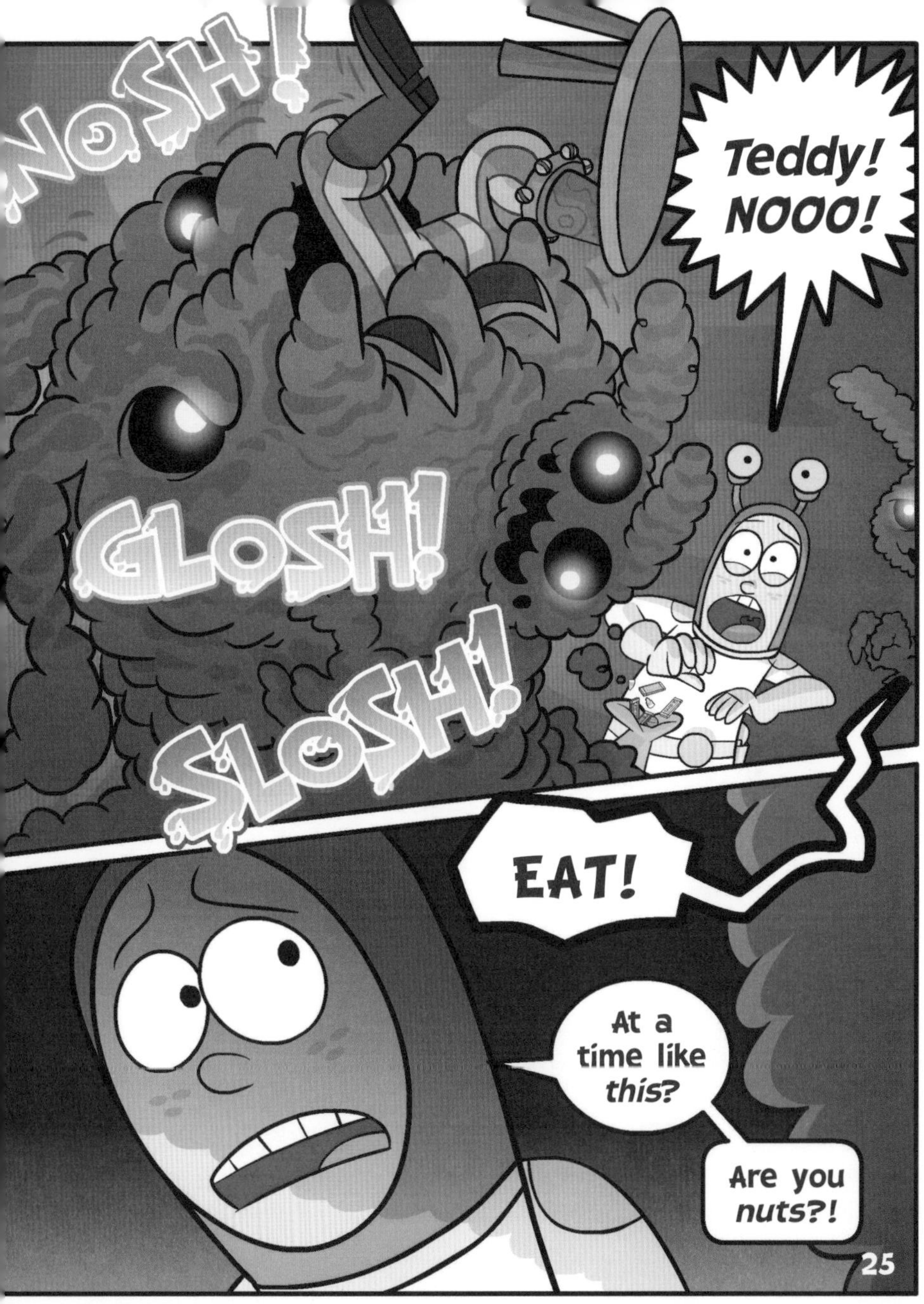
WOSH!
Teddy! NOOO!
GLOSH!
SLOSH!
EAT!
At a time like *this*?
Are you *nuts*?!

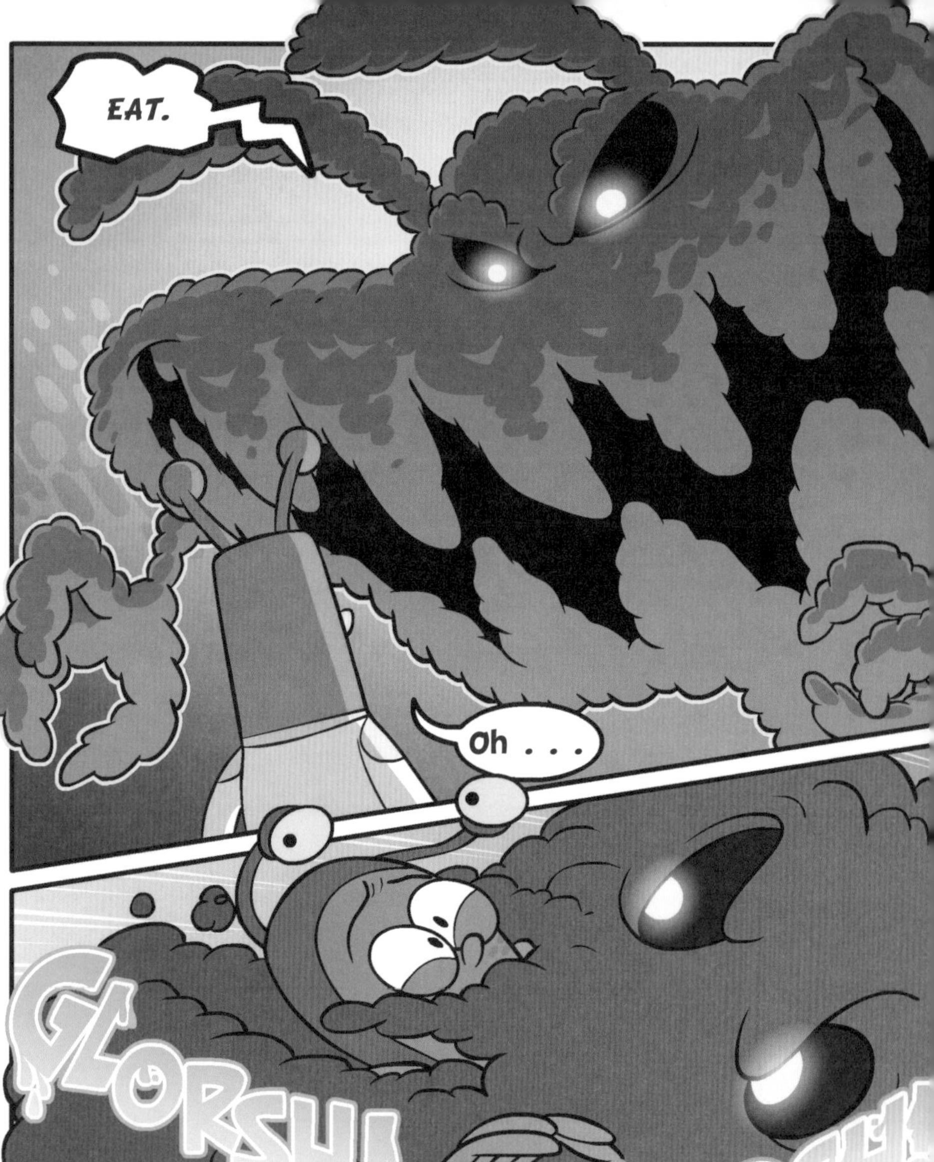
EAT.
Oh . . .
GLORSH!
GOOSH!

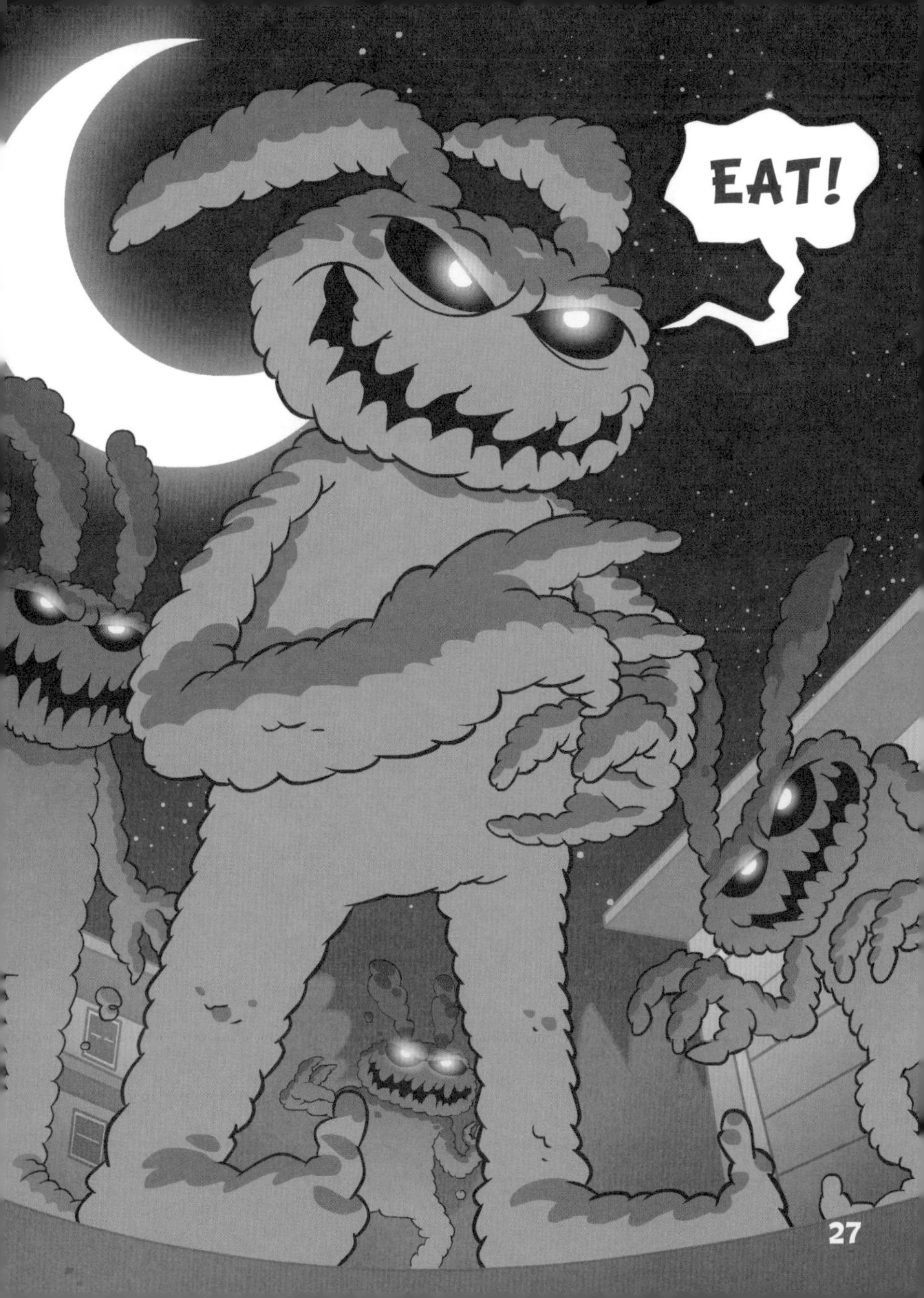
EAT!

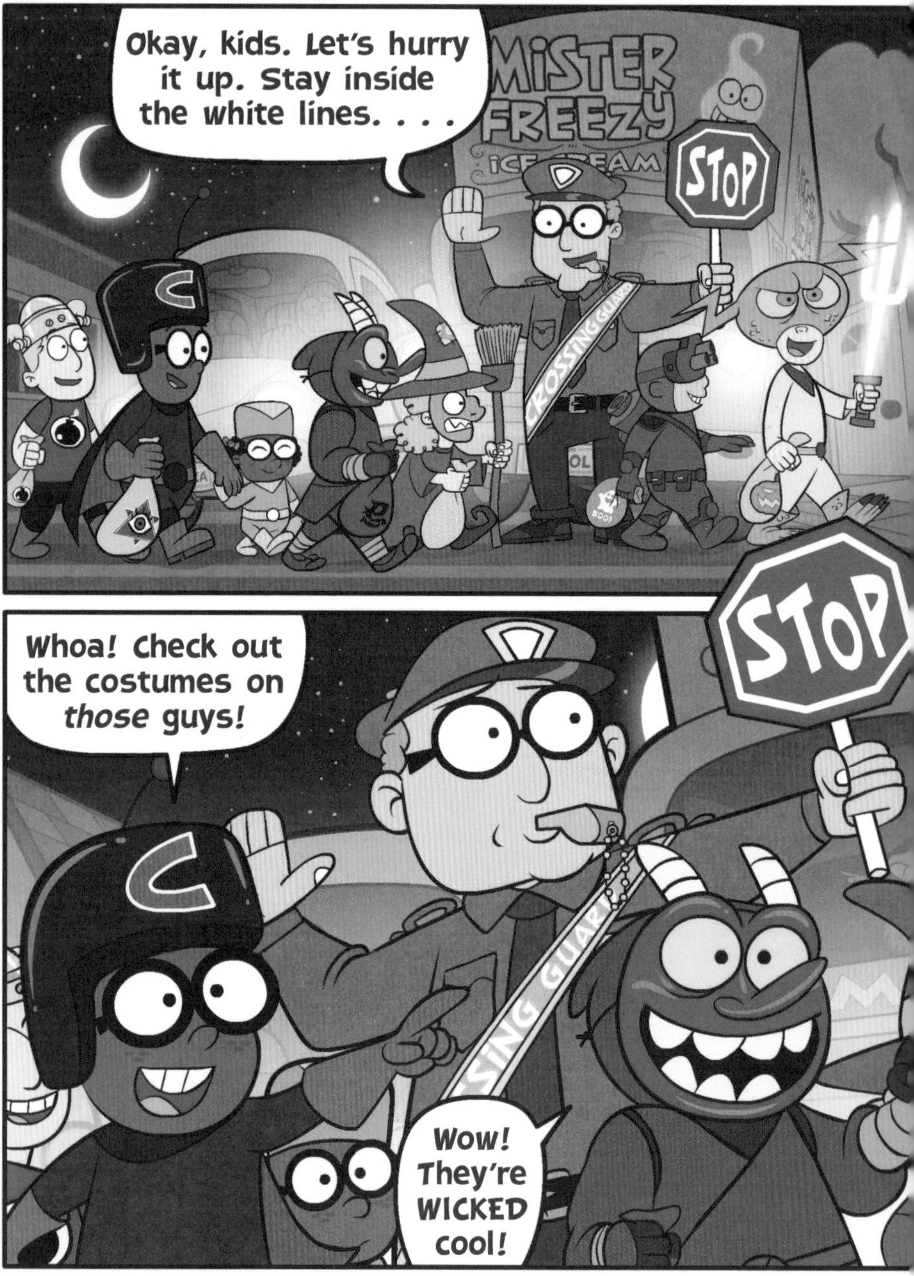
Okay, kids. Let's hurry it up. Stay inside the white lines. . . .
MISTER FREEZY ICE CREAM
STOP
CROSSING GUARD
BOO!
Whoa! Check out the costumes on *those* guys!
STOP
Wow! They're WICKED cool!

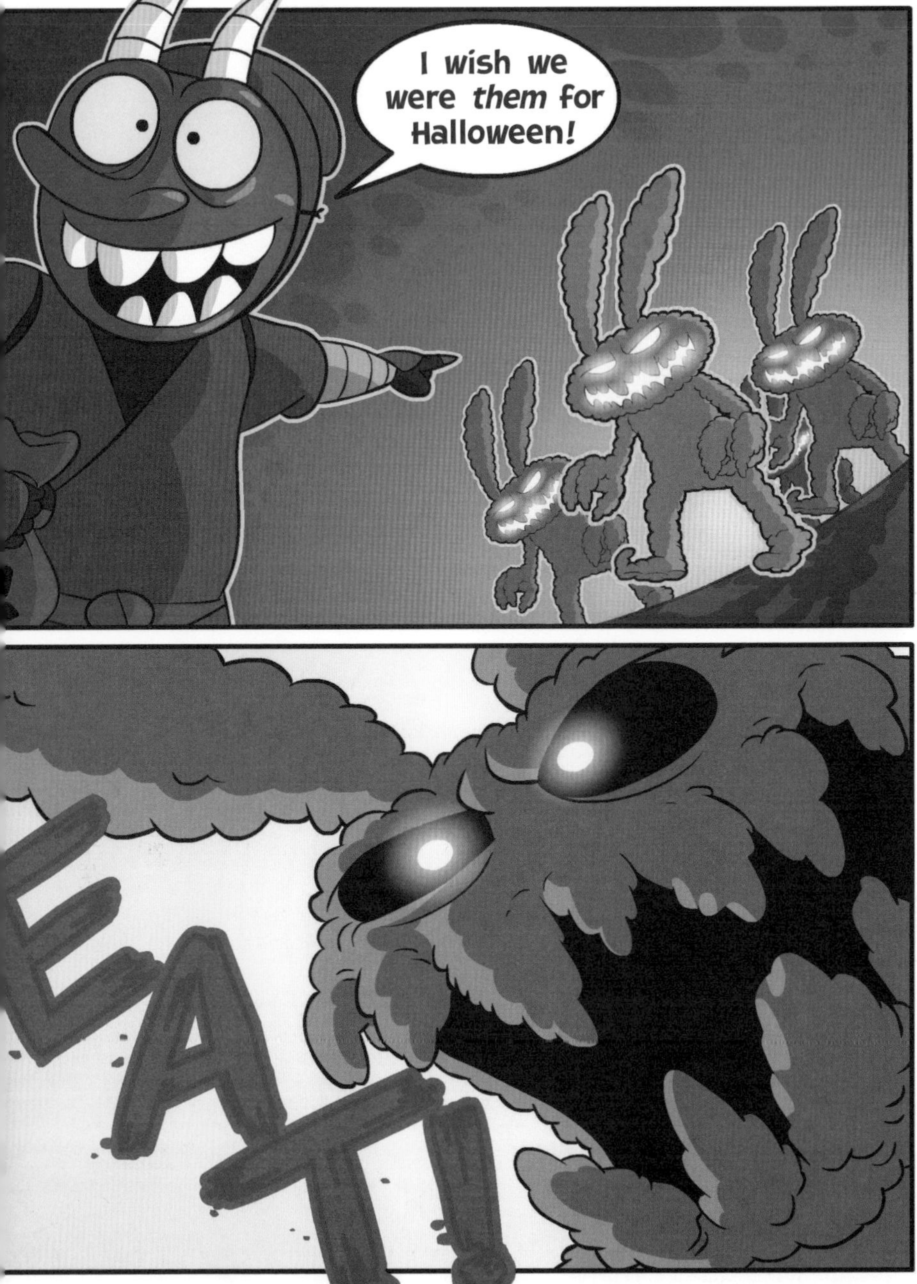
I wish we were *them* for Halloween!
EAT!

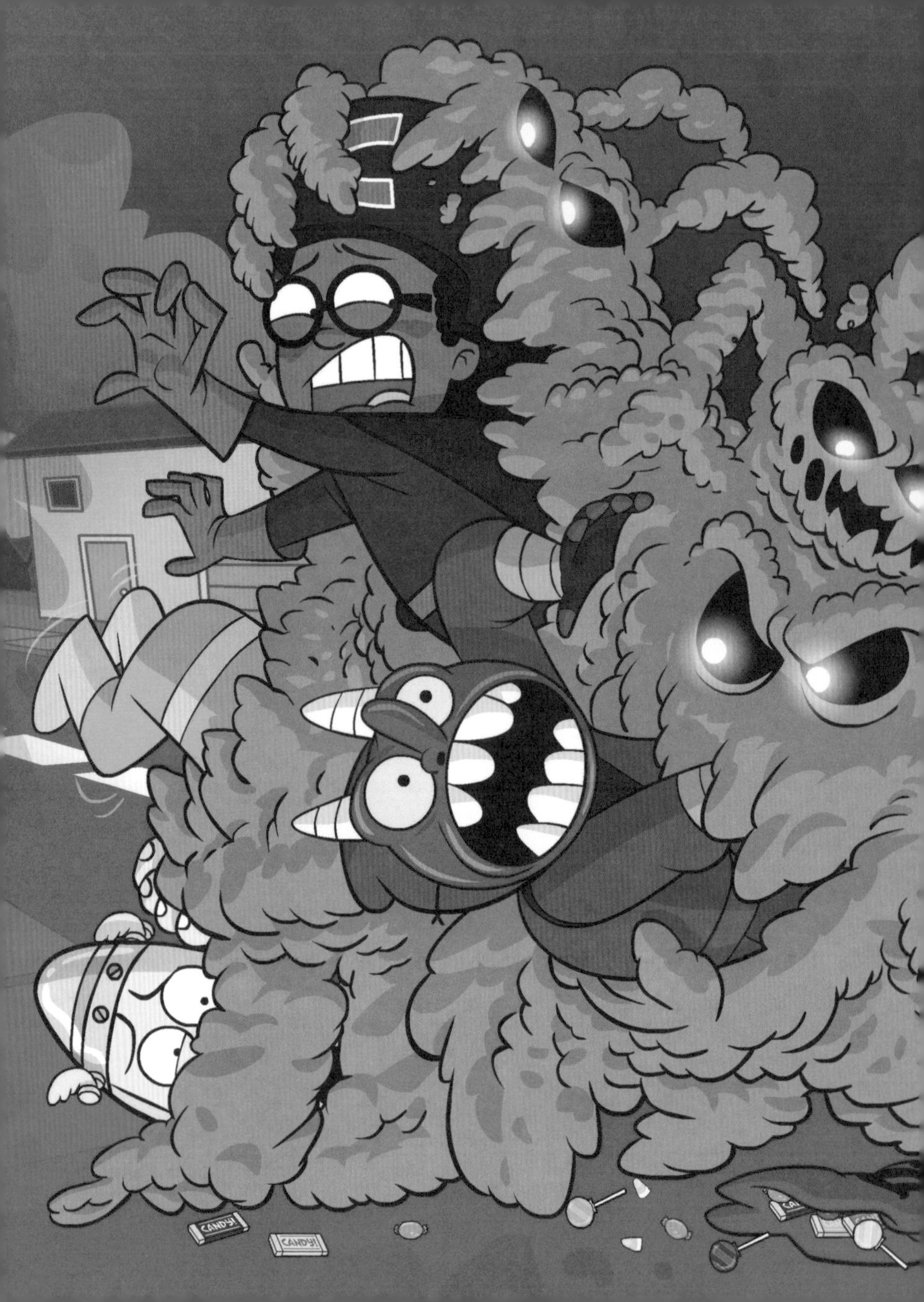
CANDY!
CANDY!

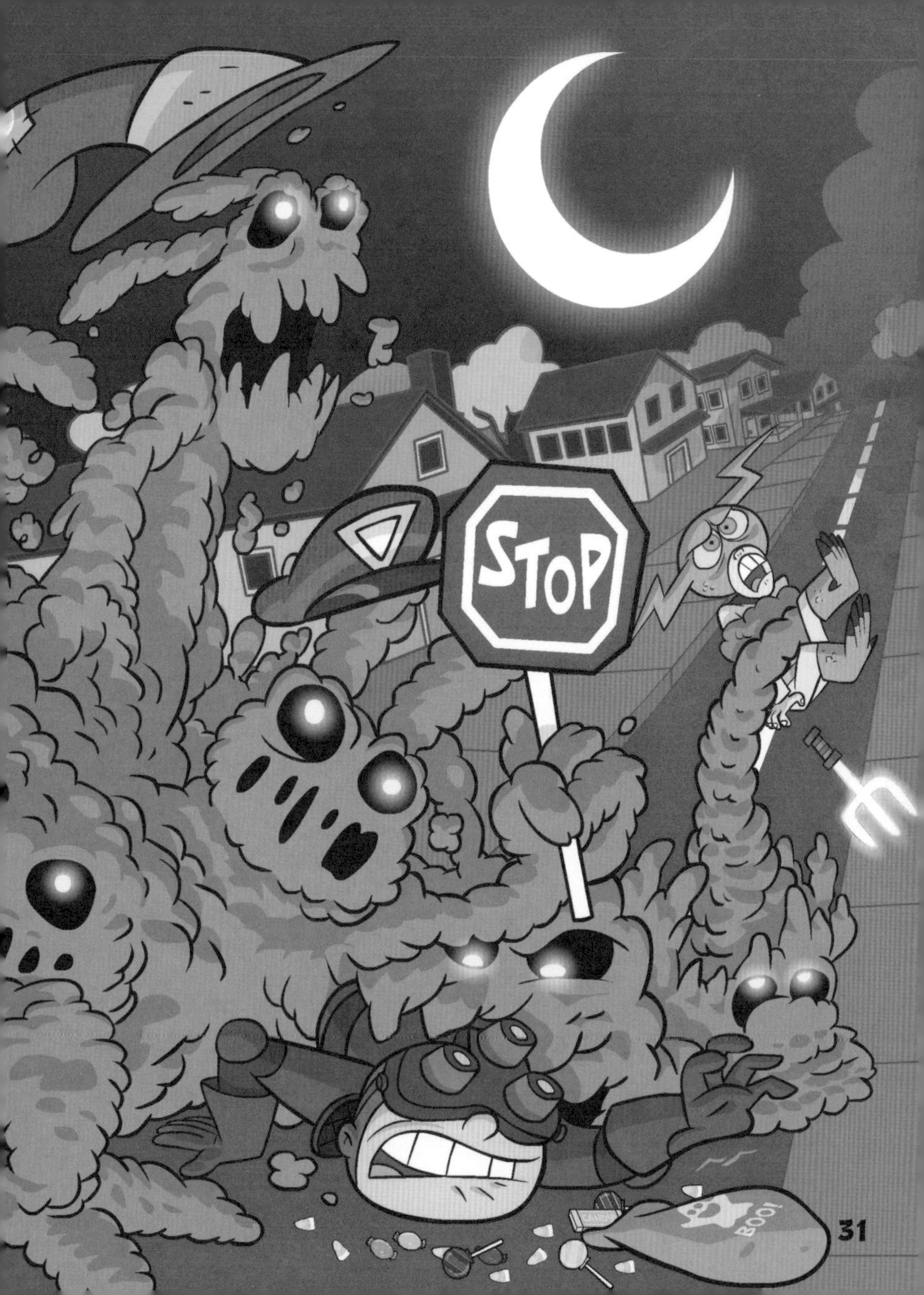
STOP
BOO!

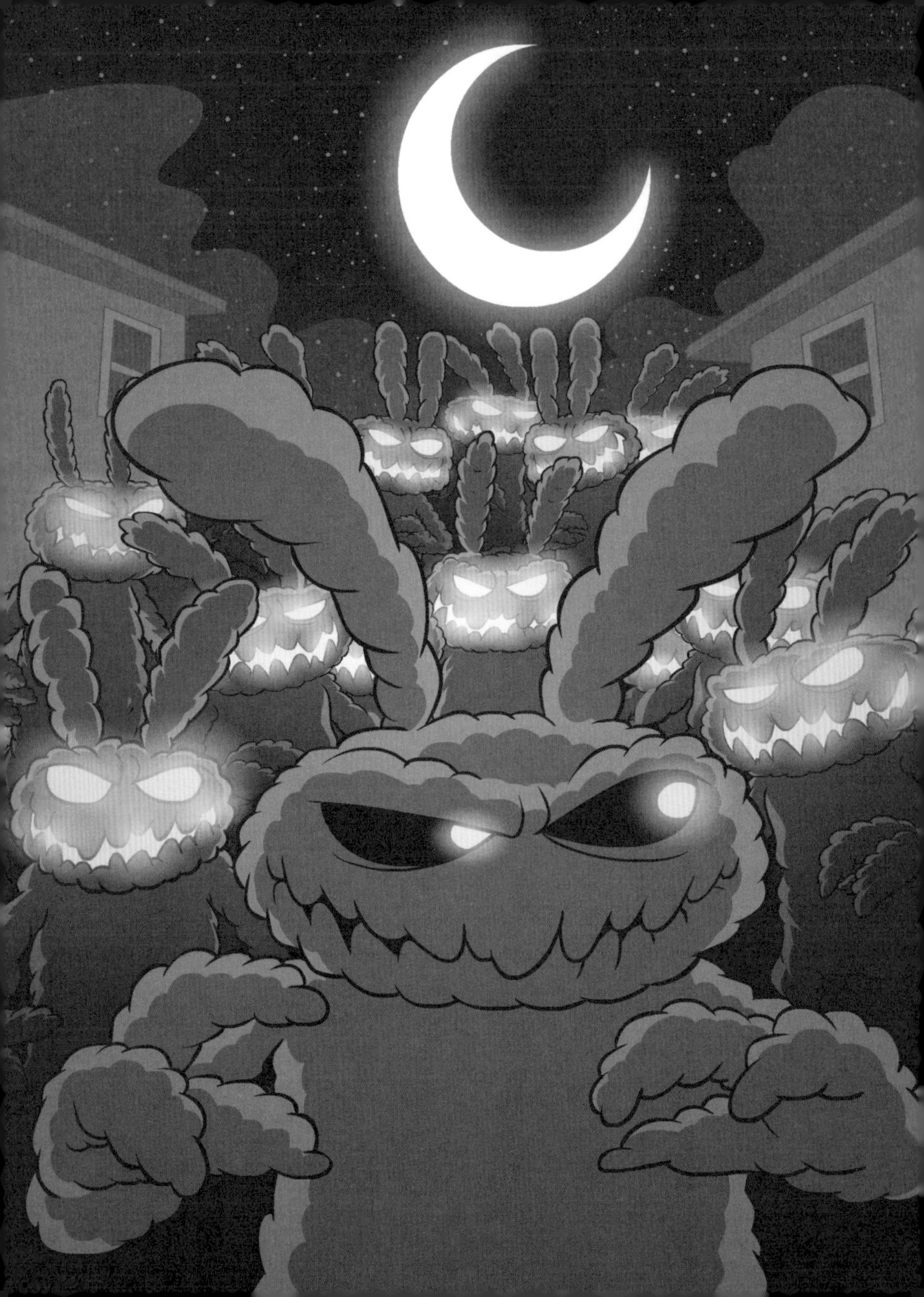

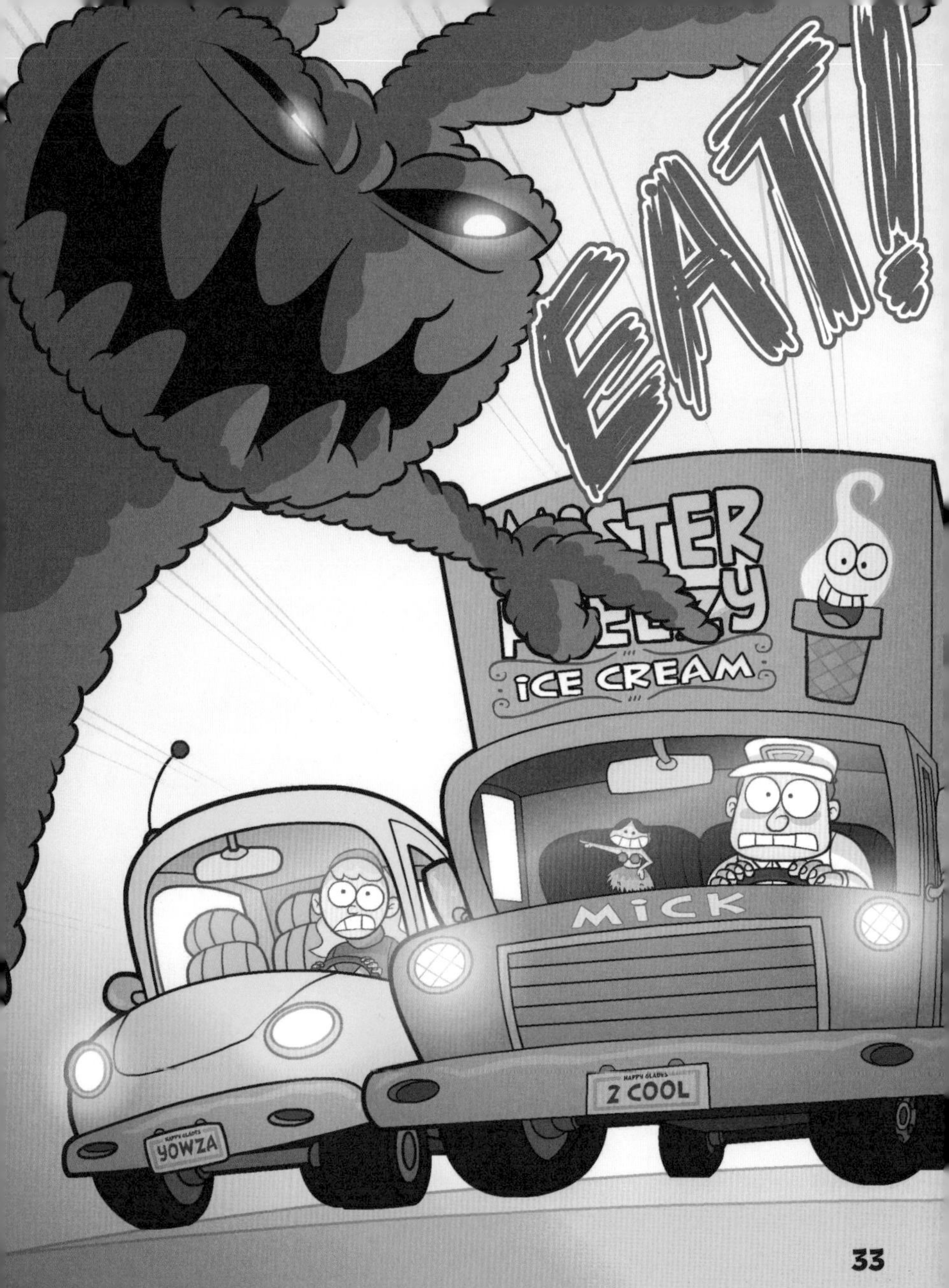
EAT!
ICE CREAM
MICK
2 COOL
YOWZA

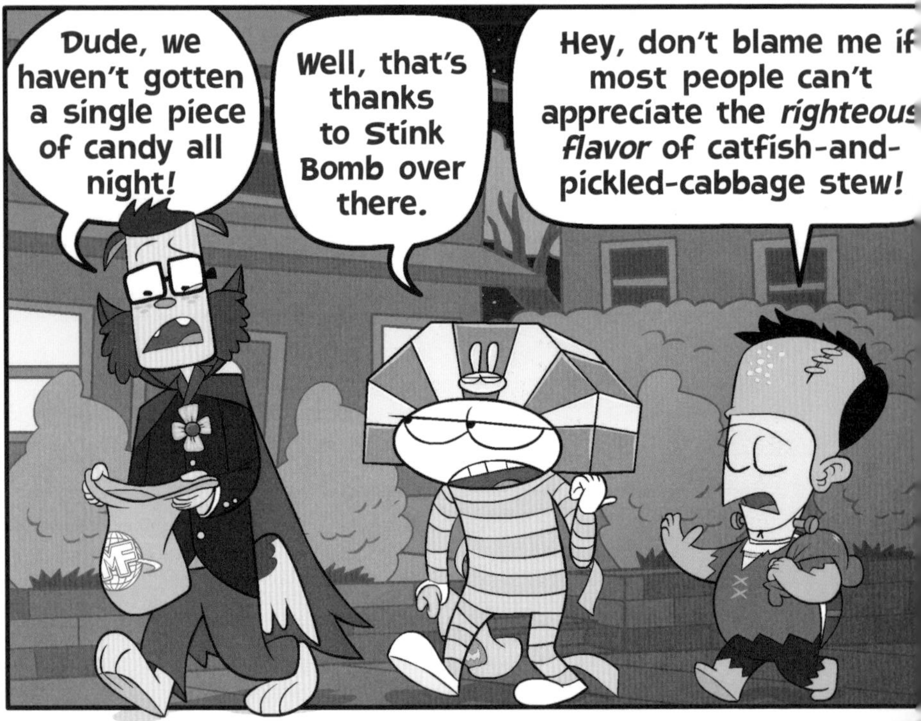
Dude, we haven't gotten a single piece of candy all night!
Well, that's thanks to Stink Bomb over there.
Hey, don't blame me if most people can't appreciate the *righteous flavor* of catfish-and-pickled-cabbage stew!

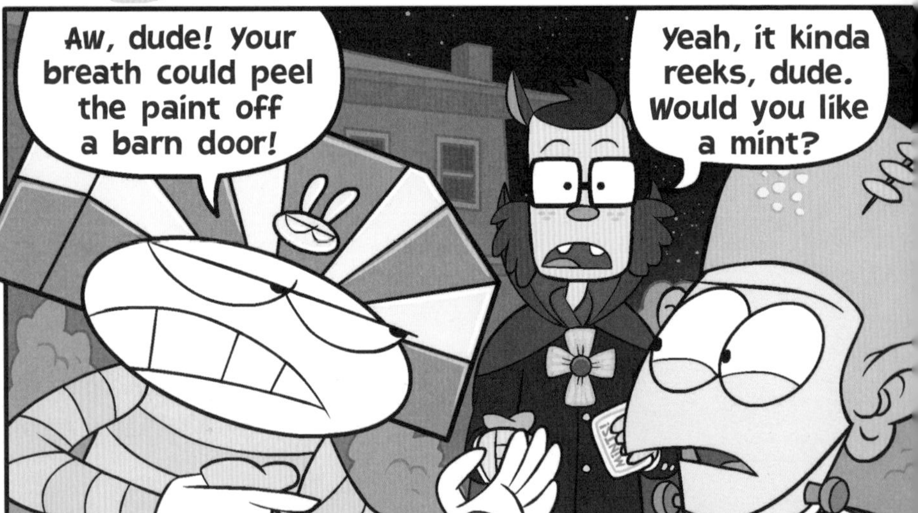
Aw, dude! Your breath could peel the paint off a barn door!
Yeah, it kinda reeks, dude. Would you like a mint?

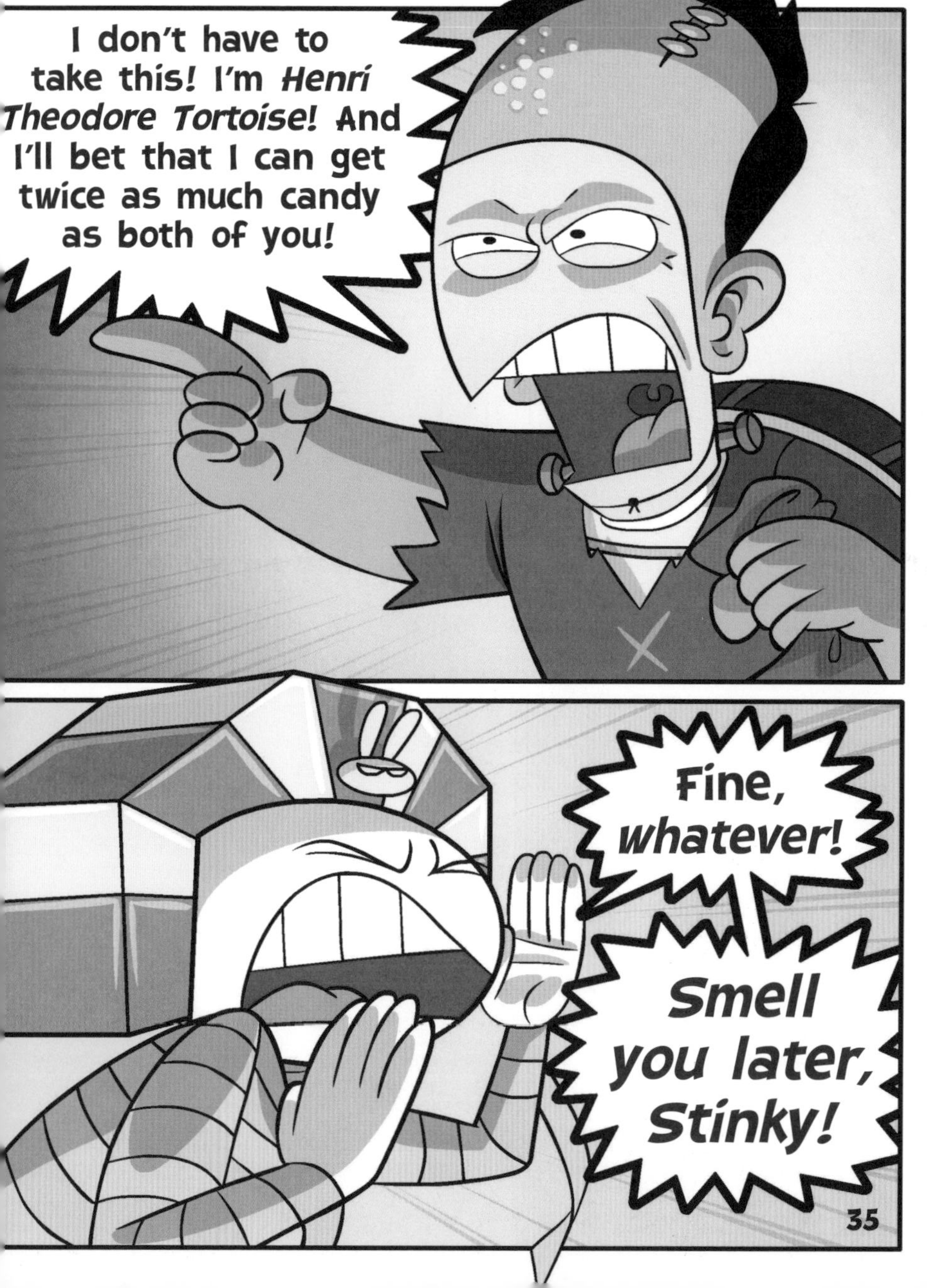
I don't have to take this! I'm *Henri Theodore Tortoise!* And I'll bet that I can get twice as much candy as both of you!
Fine, *whatever!*
Smell you later, Stinky!

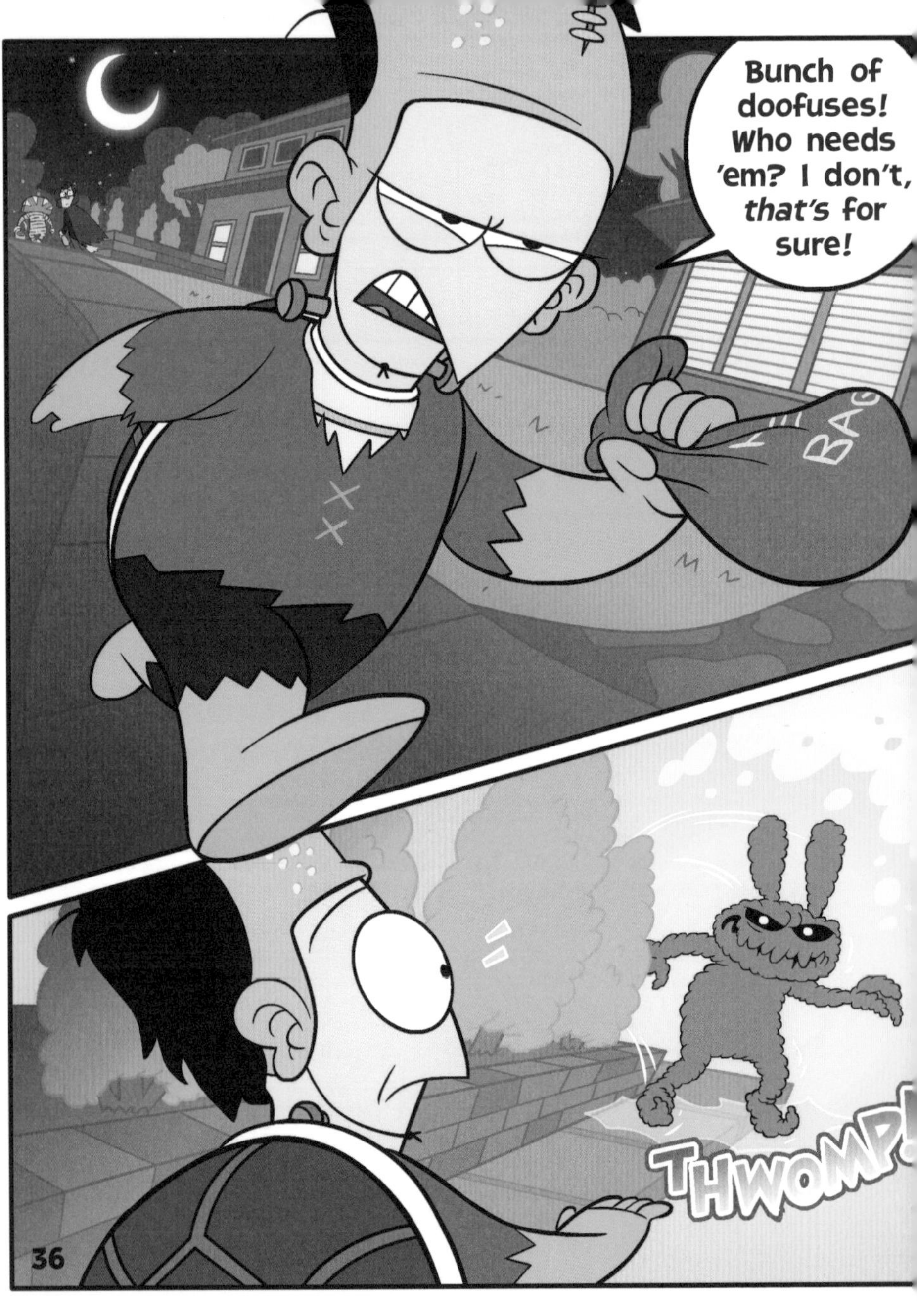
Bunch of doofuses! Who needs 'em? I don't, *that's* for sure!
BAG
THWOMP!

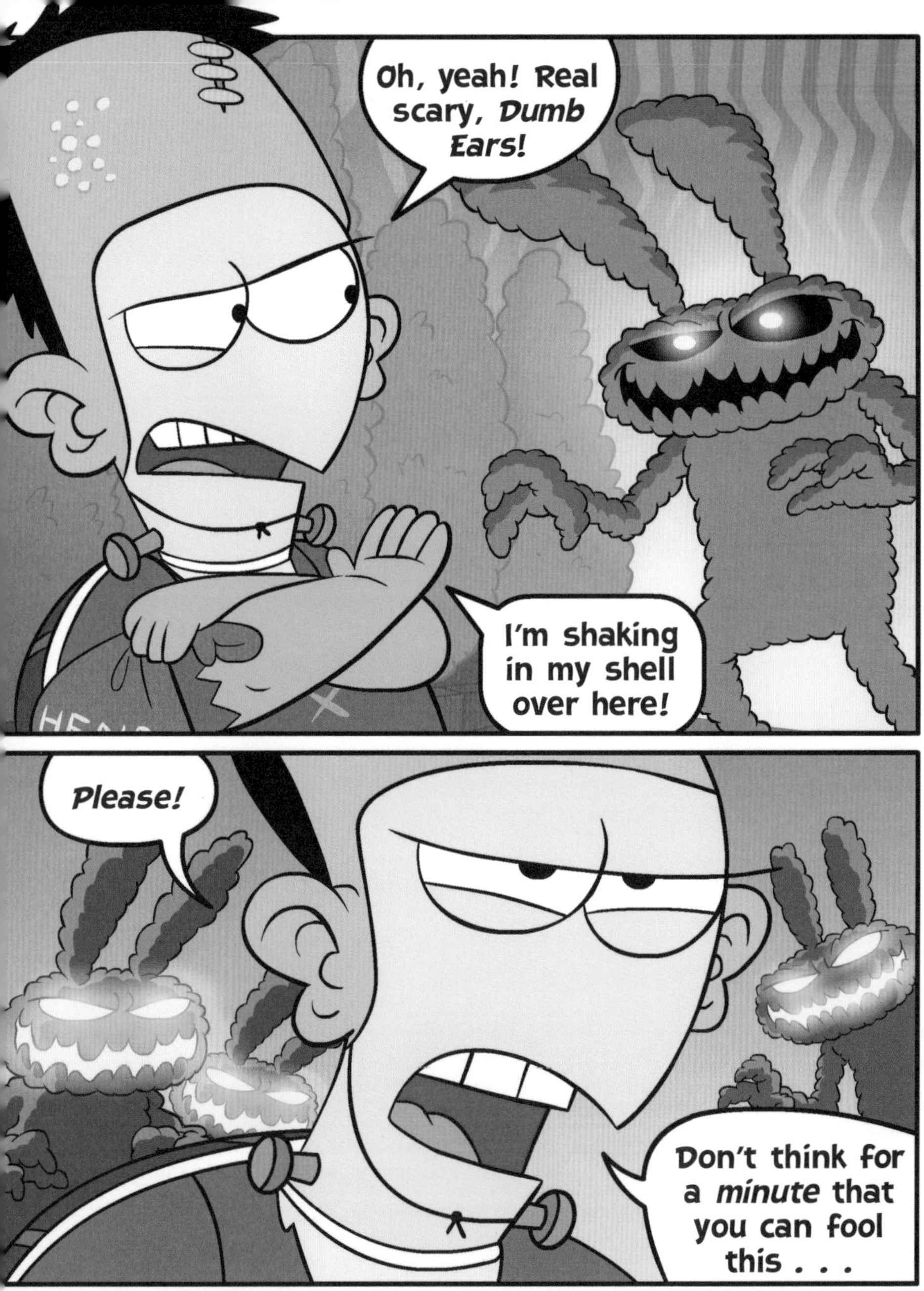
Oh, yeah! Real scary, *Dumb Ears!*
I'm shaking in my shell over here!
Please!
Don't think for a *minute* that you can fool this . . .

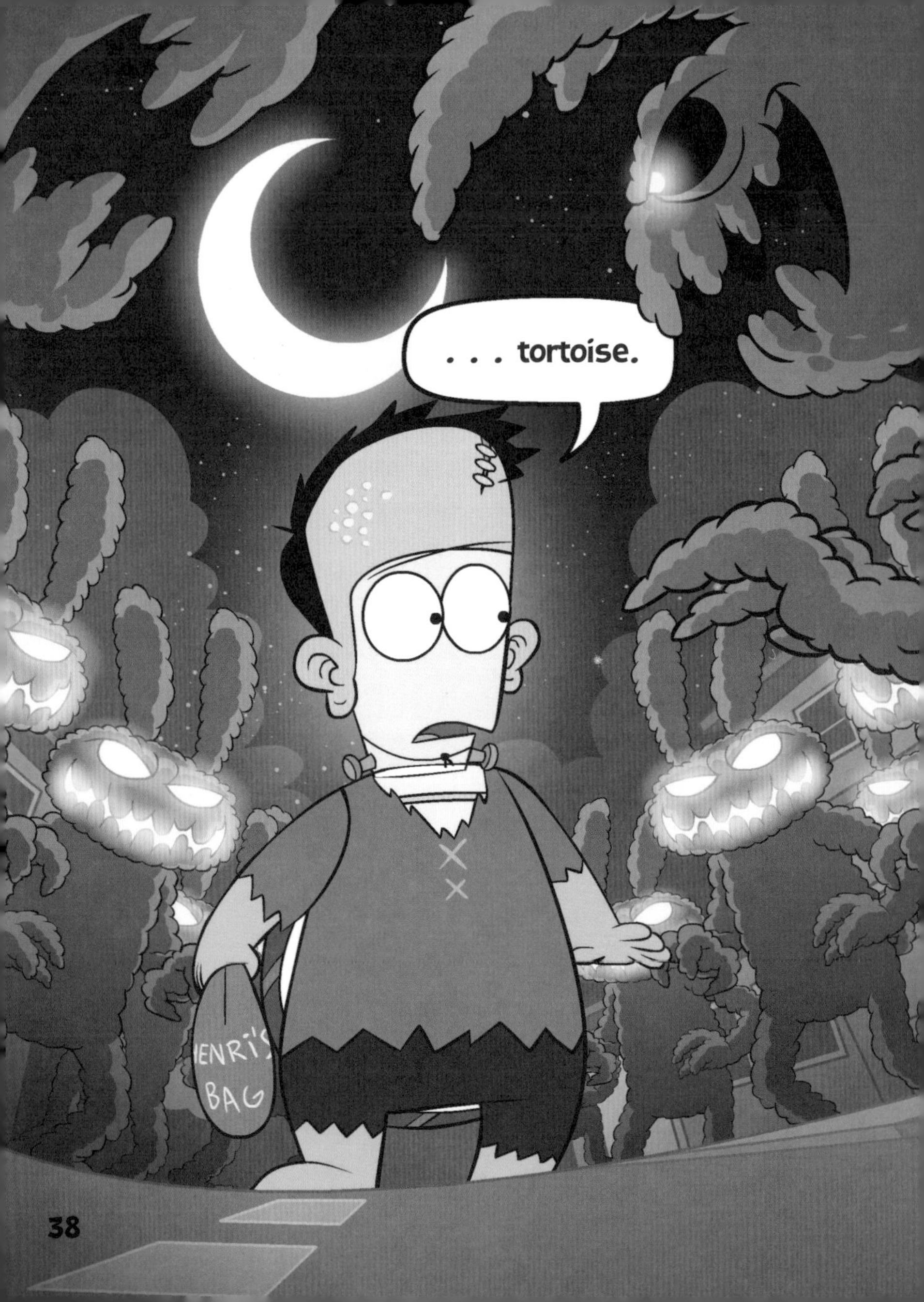
. . . tortoise.
HENRI'S BAG

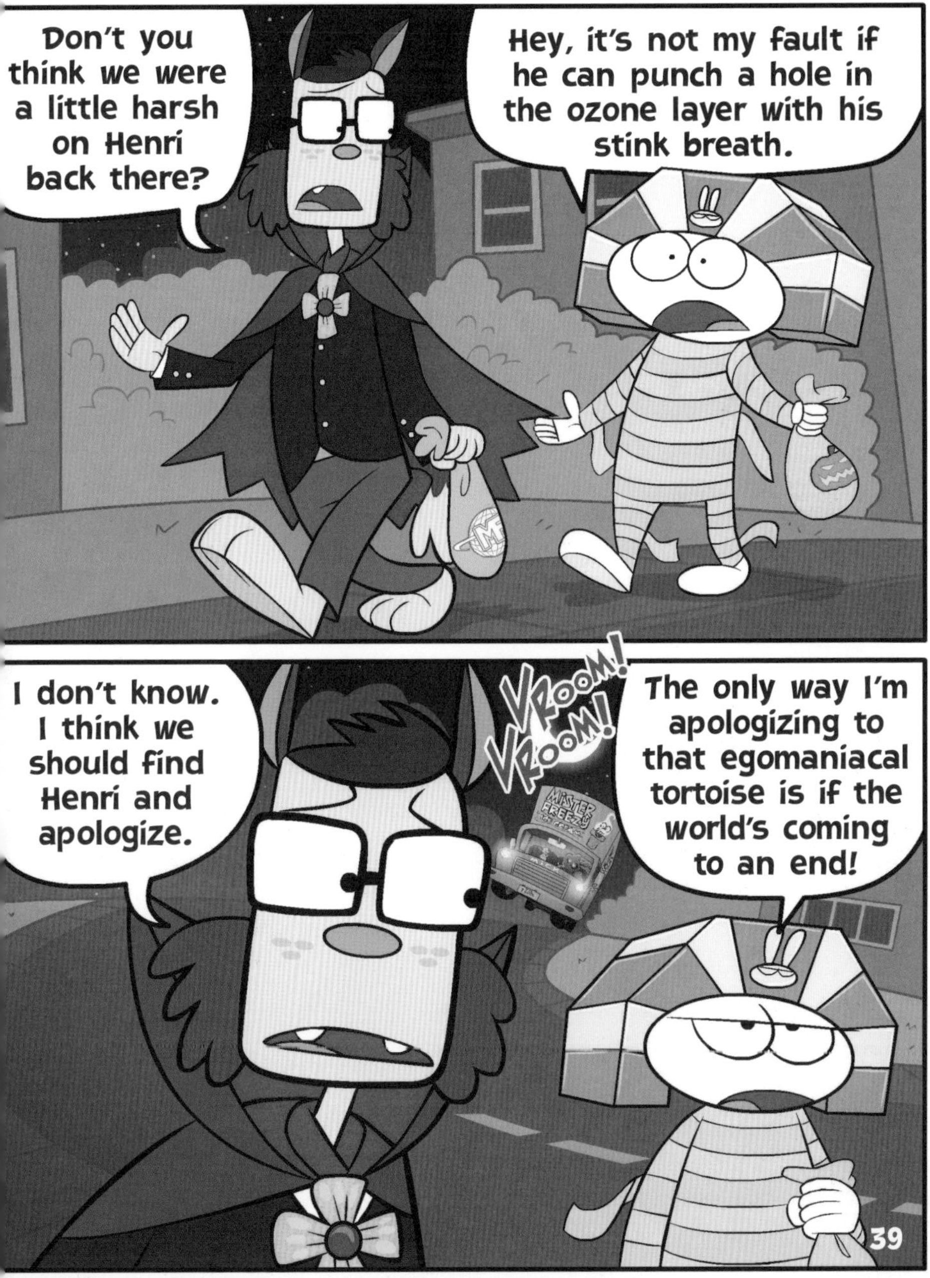
Don't you think we were a little harsh on Henri back there?
Hey, it's not my fault if he can punch a hole in the ozone layer with his stink breath.
I don't know. I think we should find Henri and apologize.
VROOM! VROOM!
MISTER FREEZY
The only way I'm apologizing to that egomaniacal tortoise is if the world's coming to an end!

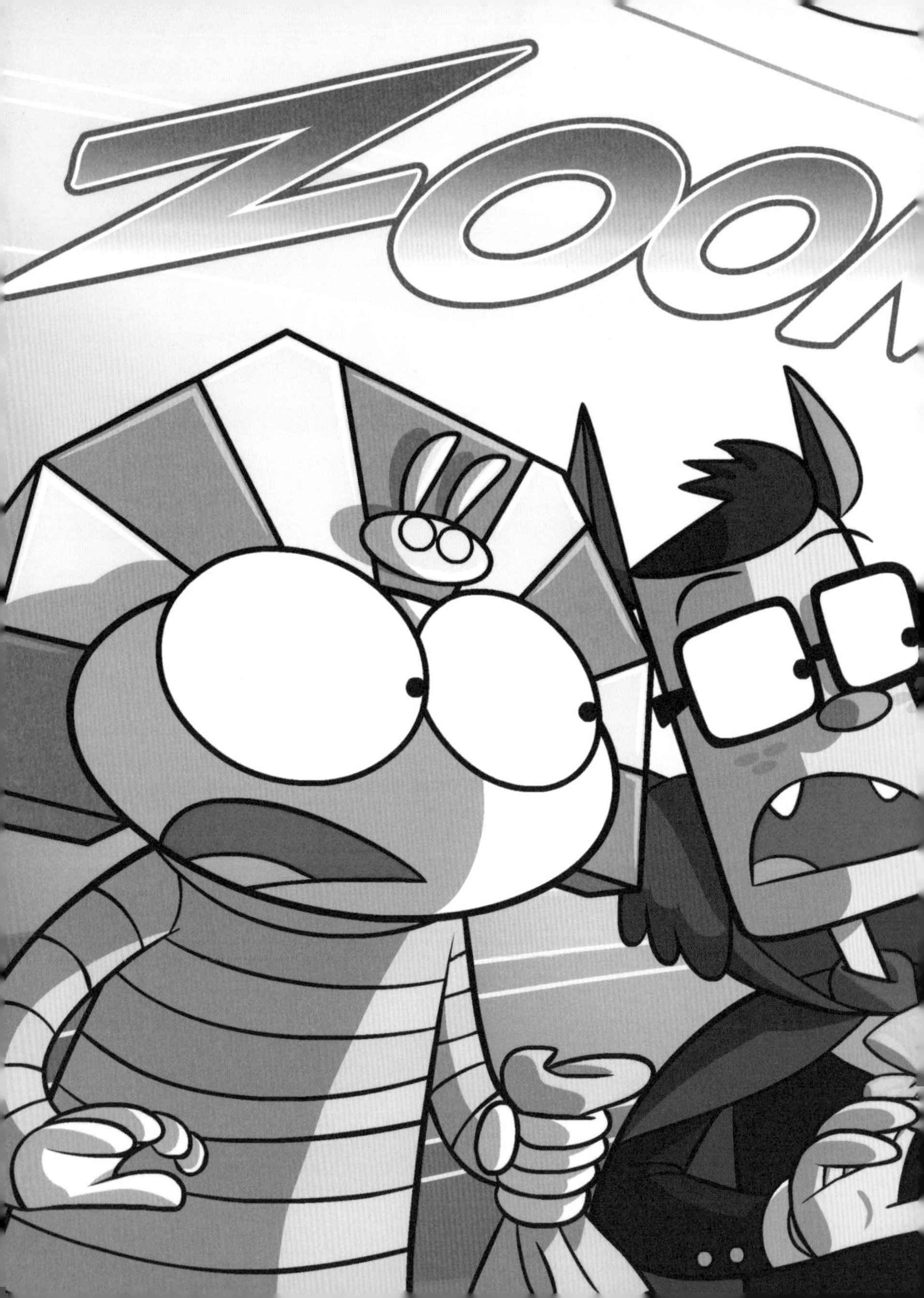
ZOO

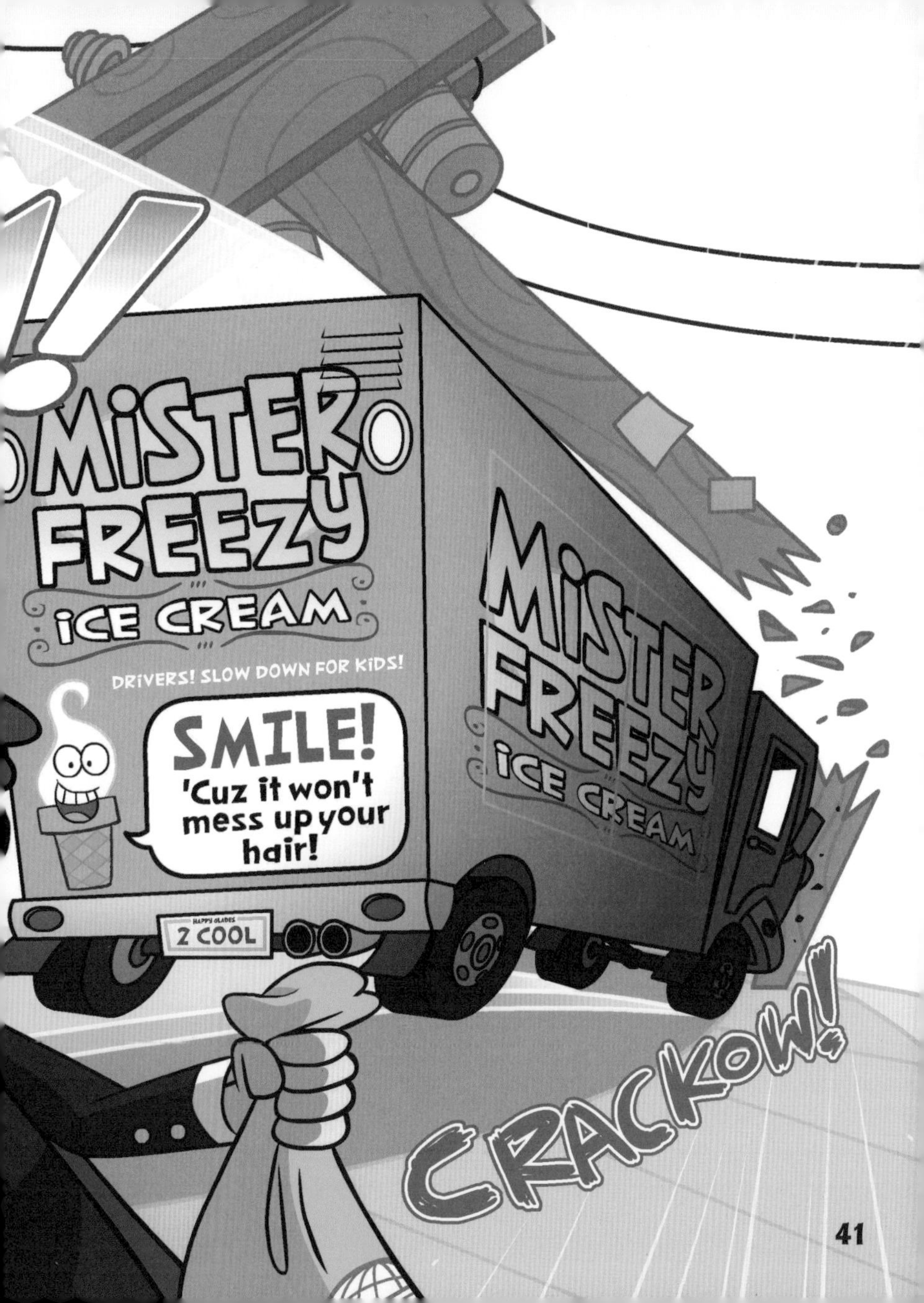
MISTER FREEZY ICE CREAM
DRIVERS! SLOW DOWN FOR KIDS!
SMILE! 'Cuz it won't mess up your hair!
HAPPY GLADES 2 COOL
MISTER FREEZY ICE CREAM
CRACKOW!

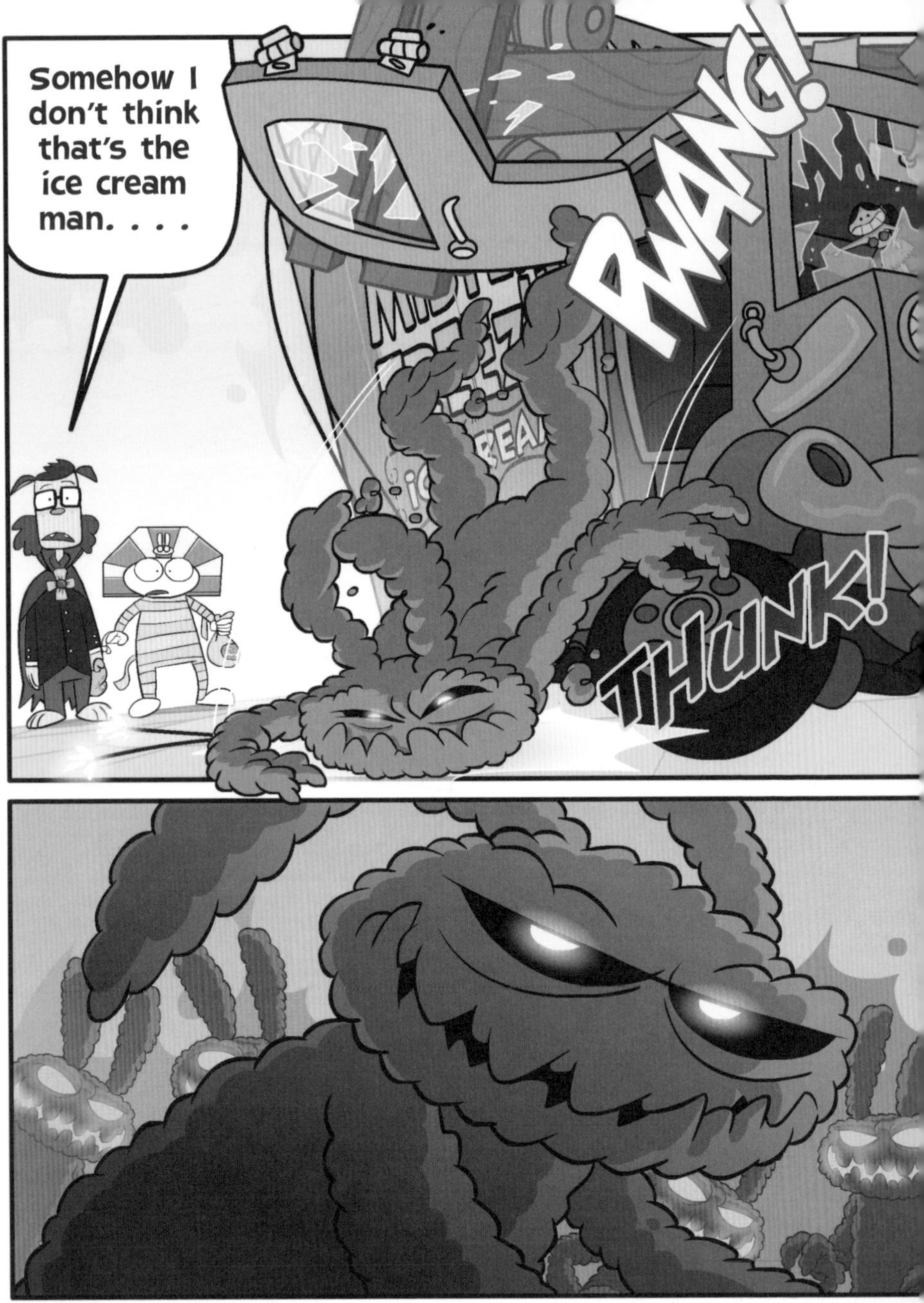
Somehow I don't think that's the ice cream man. . . .
RWANG!
THUNK!

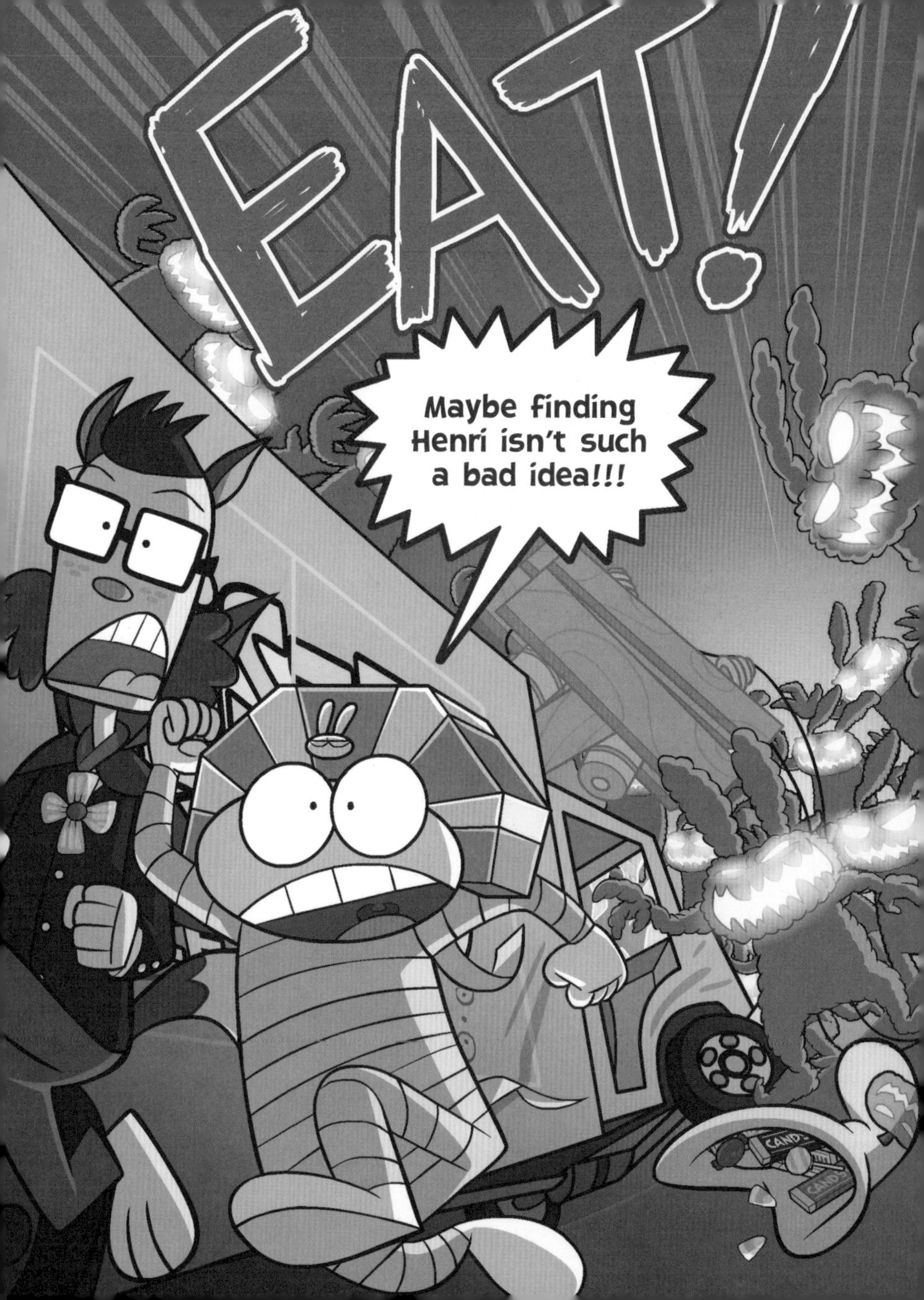
EAT!
Maybe finding Henri isn't such a bad idea!!!

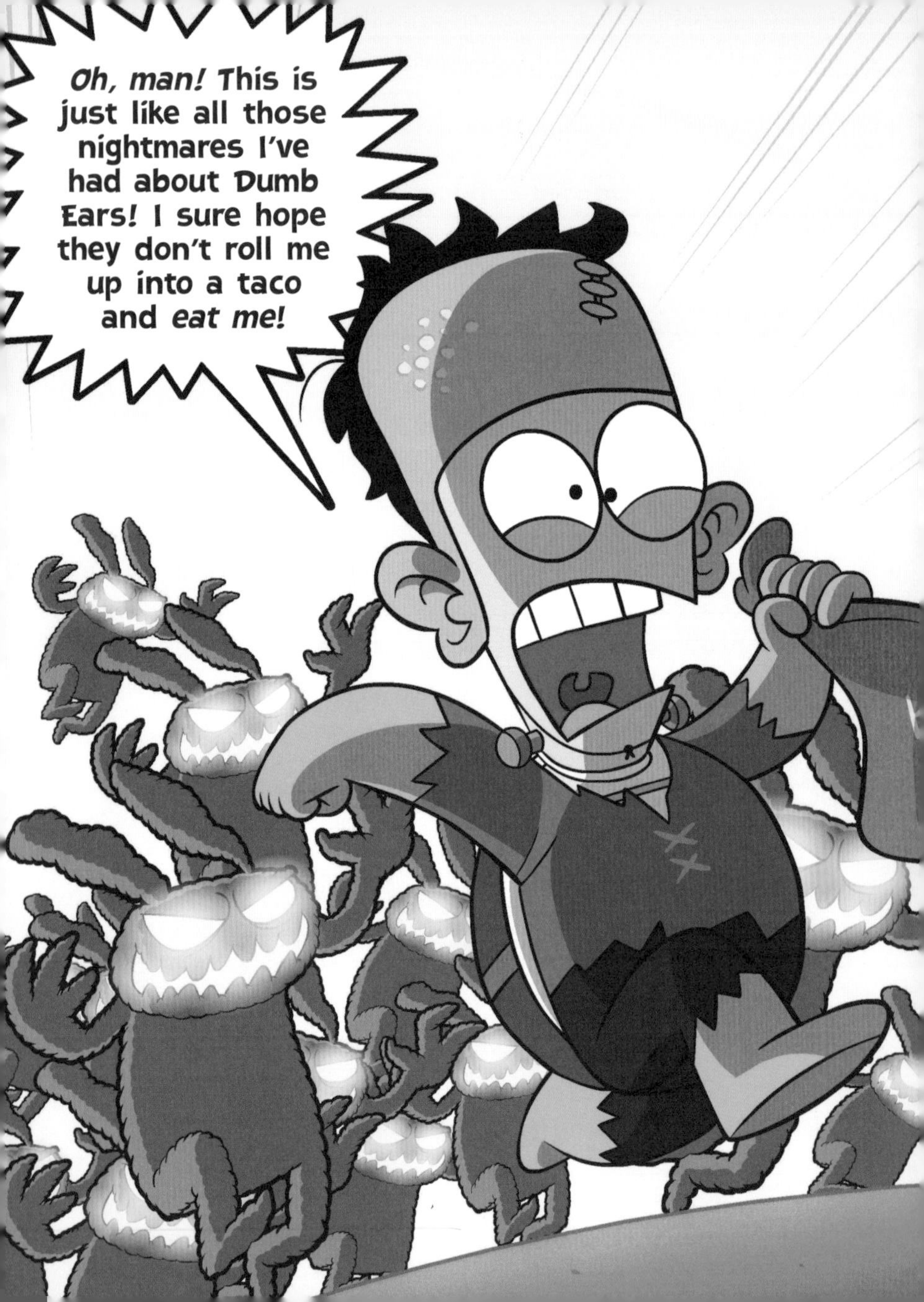
Oh, man! This is just like all those nightmares I've had about Dumb Ears! I sure hope they don't roll me up into a taco and *eat me!*

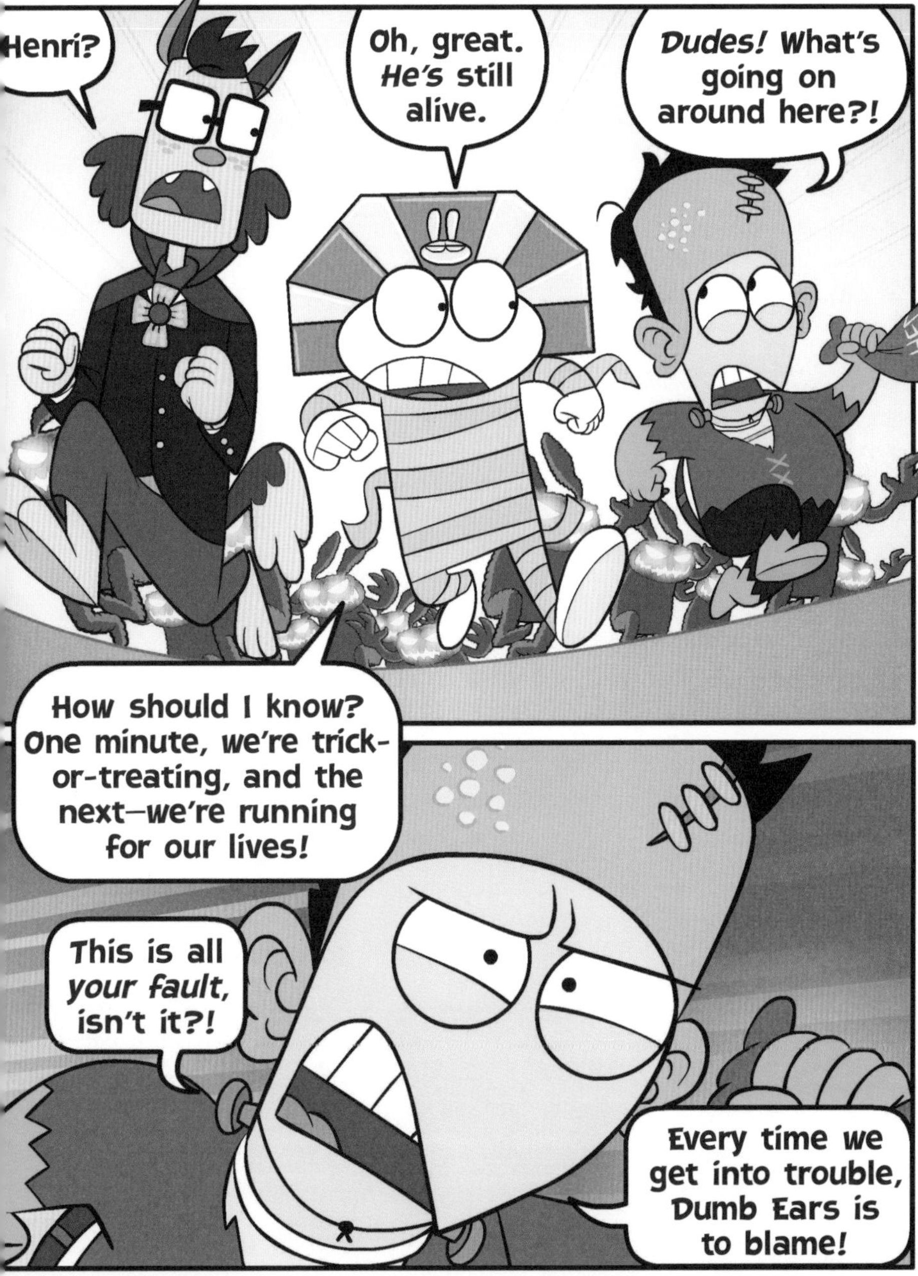
Henri?
Oh, great. *He's* still alive.
Dudes! What's going on around here?!
How should I know? One minute, we're trick-or-treating, and the next—we're running for our lives!
This is all *your fault*, isn't it?!
Every time we get into trouble, Dumb Ears is to blame!

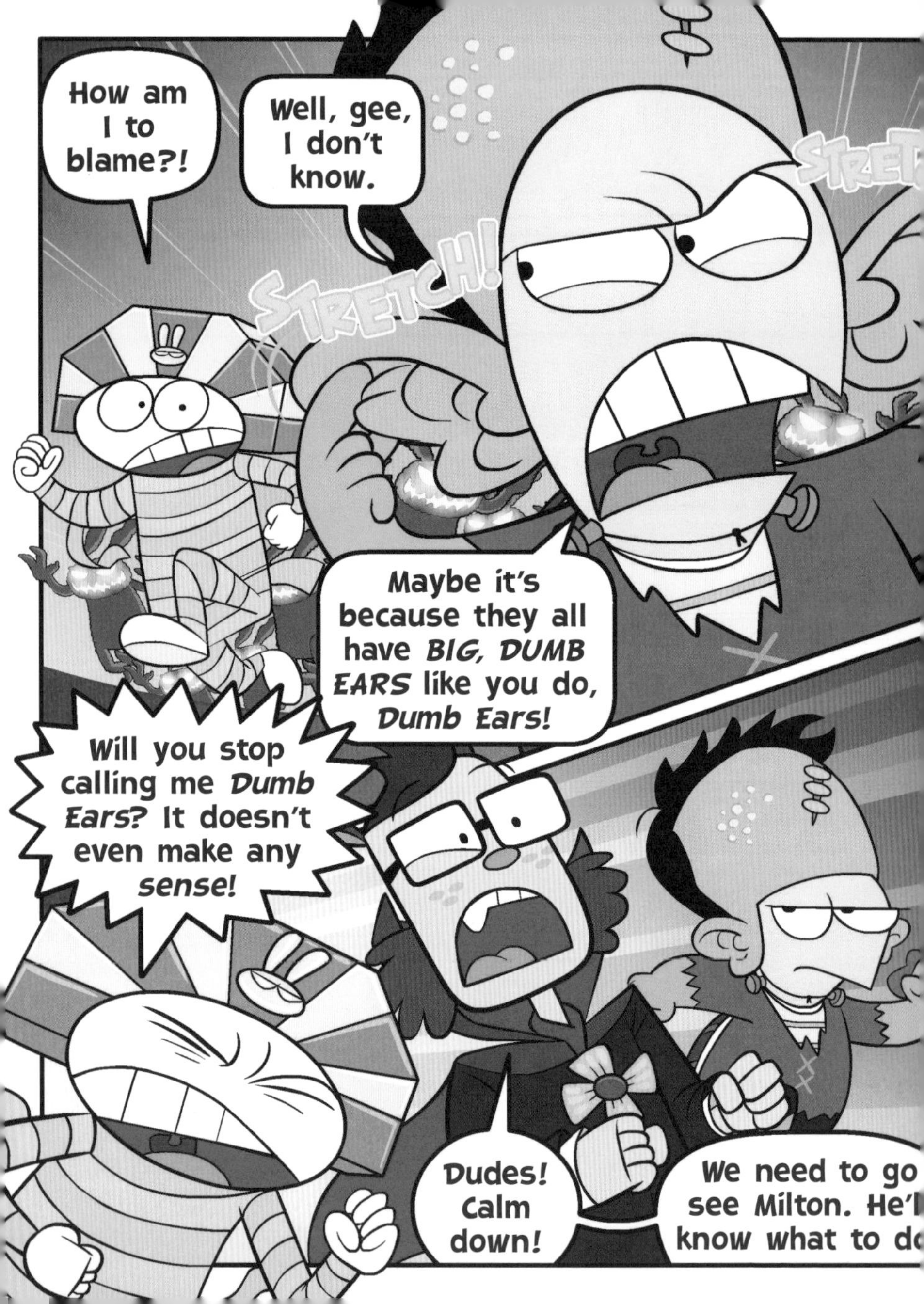
How am I to blame?!
Well, gee, I don't know.
STRETCH!
STRETCH
Maybe it's because they all have *BIG, DUMB EARS* like you do, *Dumb Ears!*
Will you stop calling me *Dumb Ears?* It doesn't even make any *sense!*
Dudes! Calm down!
We need to go see Milton. He'l know what to do

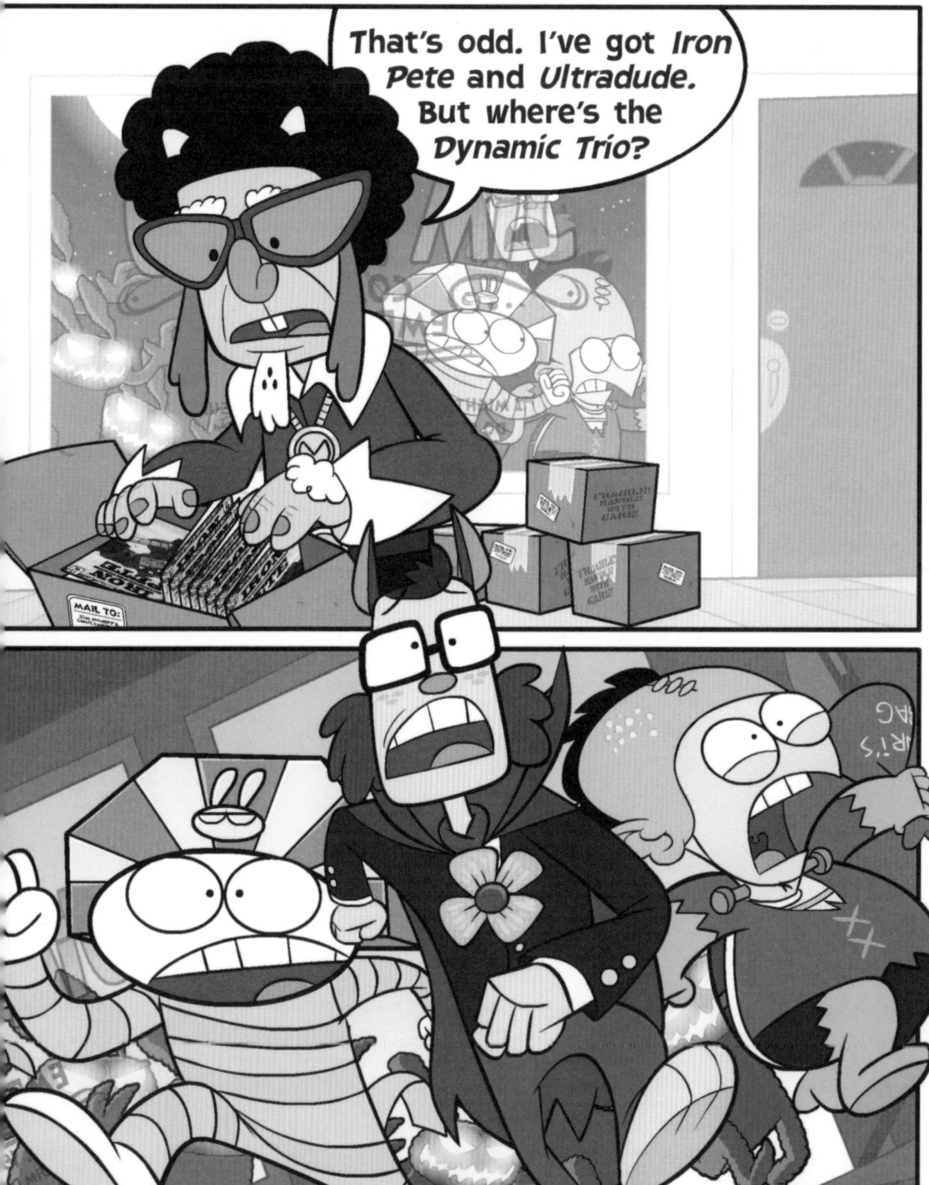
That's odd. I've got *Iron Pete* and *Ultradude.* But where's the *Dynamic Trio?*
MAIL TO:
FRAGILE! HANDLE WITH CARE!

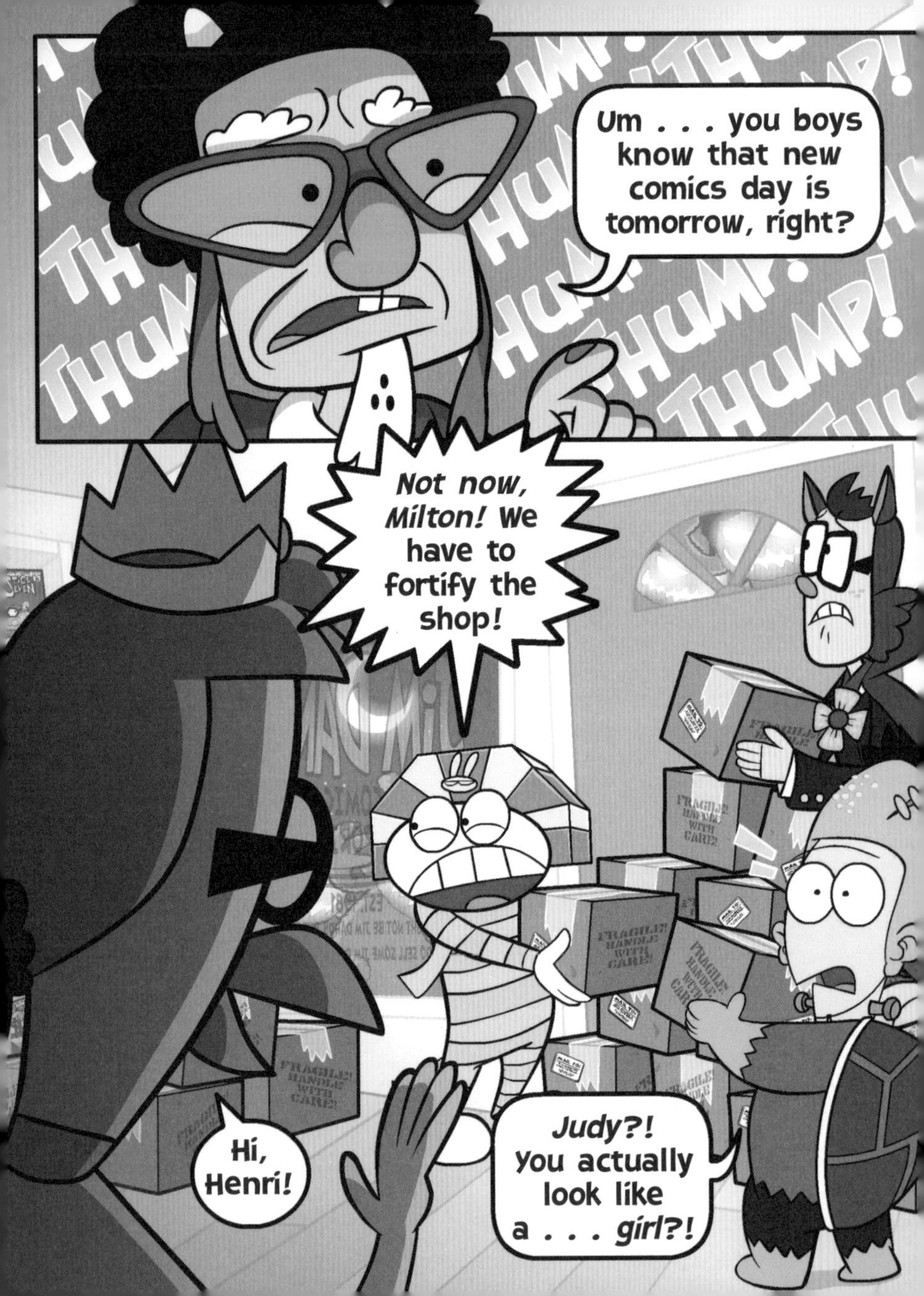
THUMP! THUMP! THUMP! THUMP!
Um . . . you boys know that new comics day is tomorrow, right?
Not now, Milton! We have to fortify the shop!
Hi, Henri!
Judy?! You actually look like a . . . girl?!
FRAGILE! HANDLE WITH CARE!

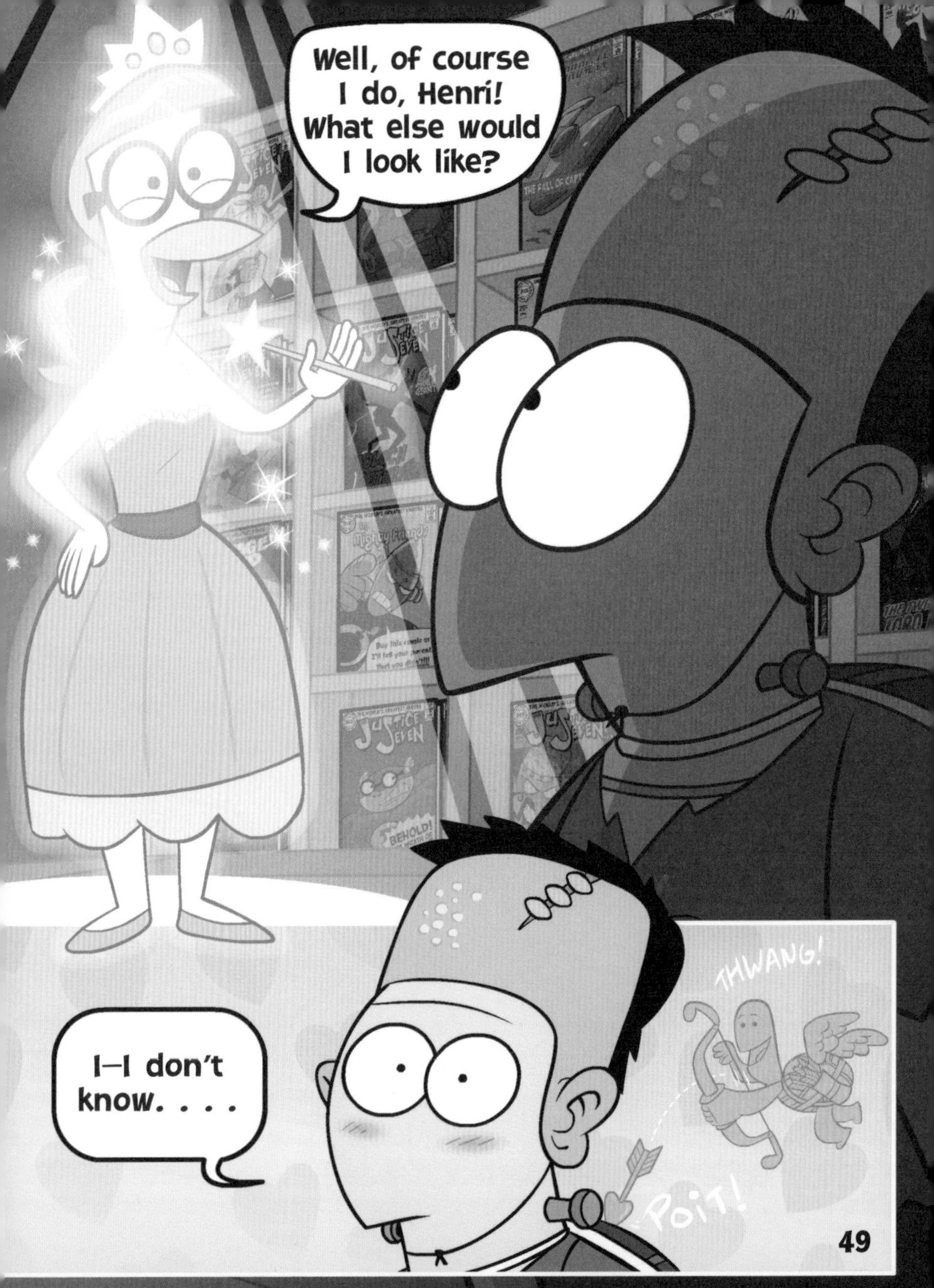
Well, of course I do, Henri! What else would I look like?
I–I don't know. . . .
THWANG!
POIT!

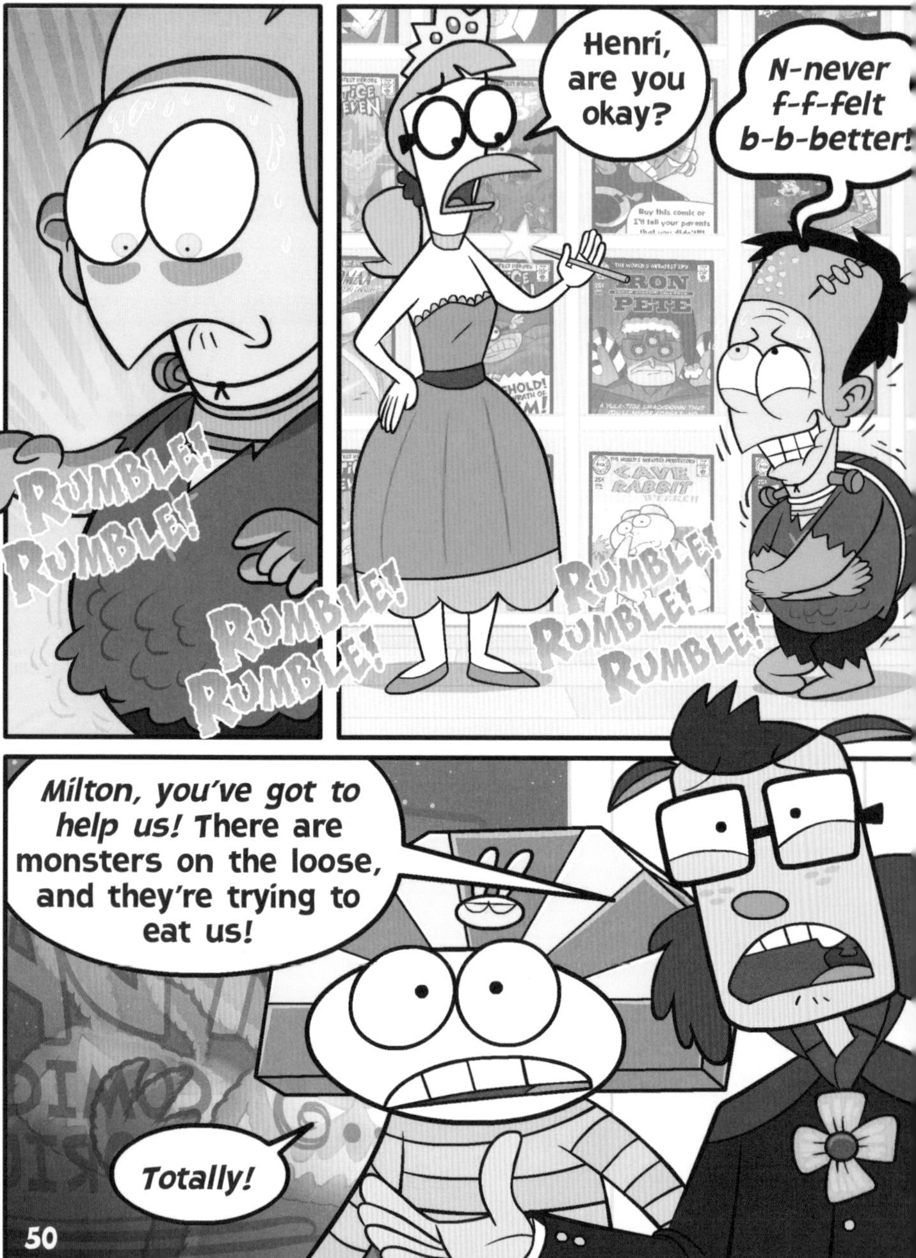

Henri, are you okay?
N-never f-f-felt b-b-better!
IRON PETE
CAVE RABBIT
Buy this comic or I'll tell your parents
RUMBLE! RUMBLE!
RUMBLE! RUMBLE!
RUMBLE! RUMBLE! RUMBLE!
Milton, you've got to help us! There are monsters on the loose, and they're trying to eat us!
Totally!

51

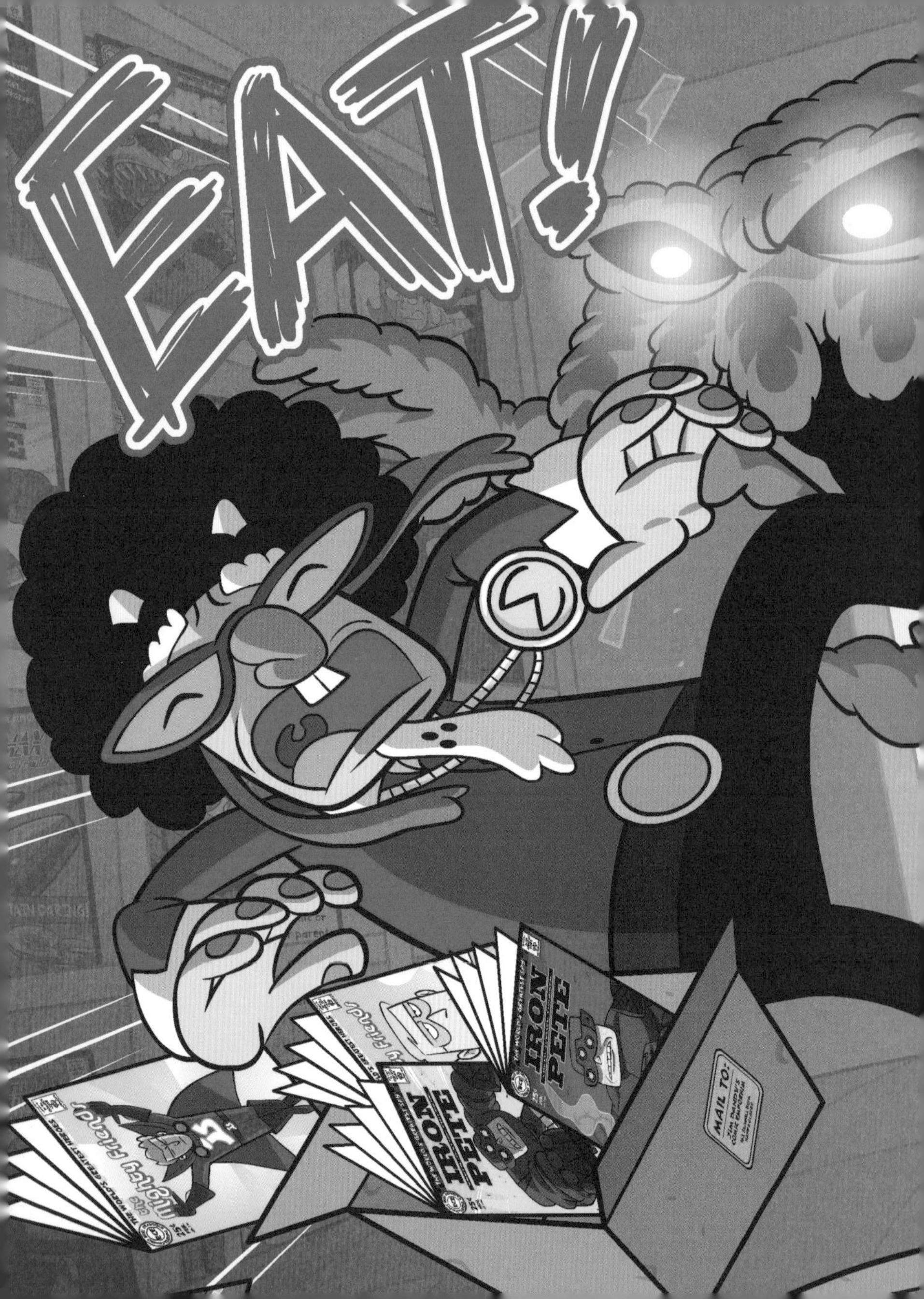
EAT!
IRON PETE
IRON PETE
MAIL TO:

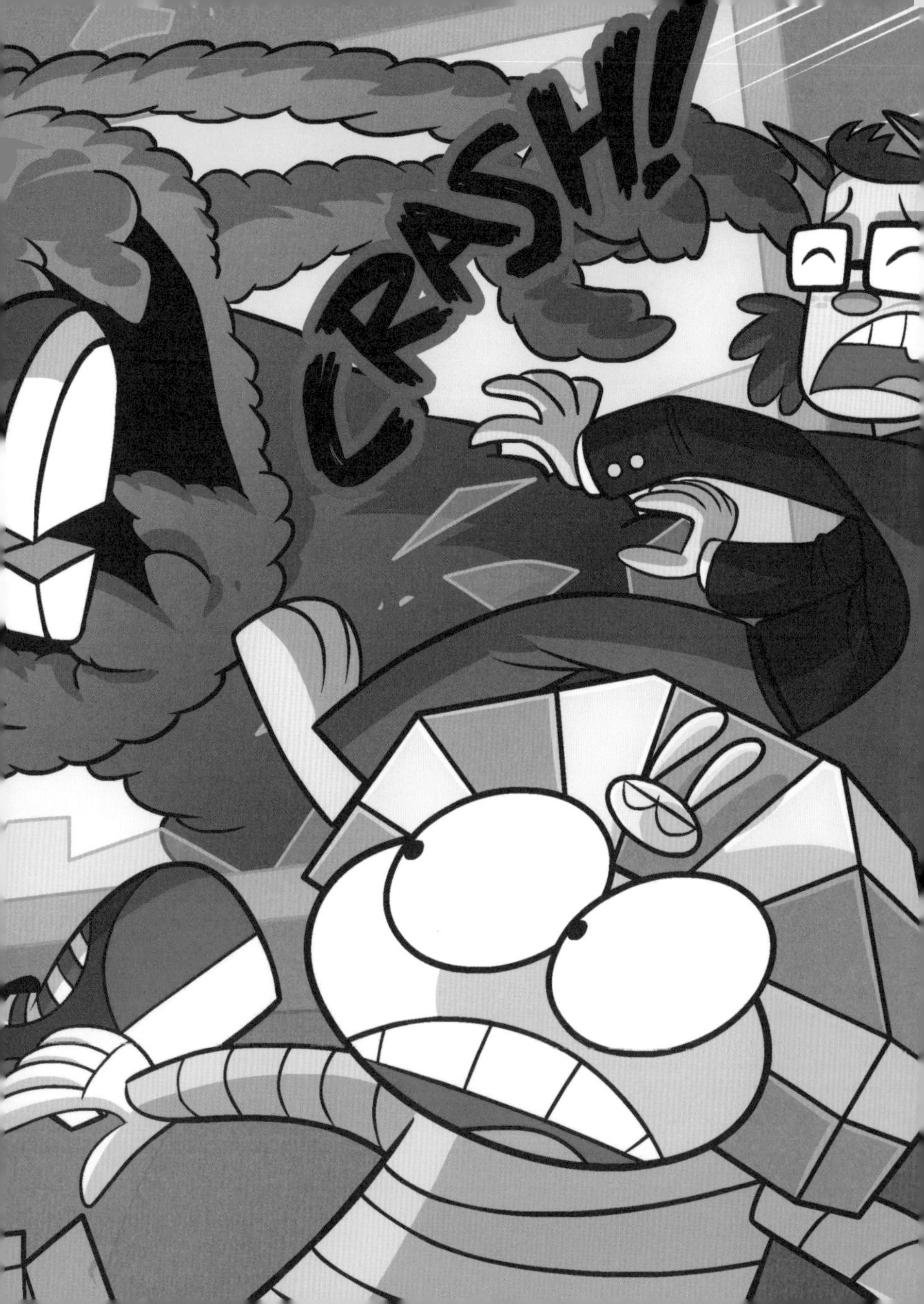
CRASH!!

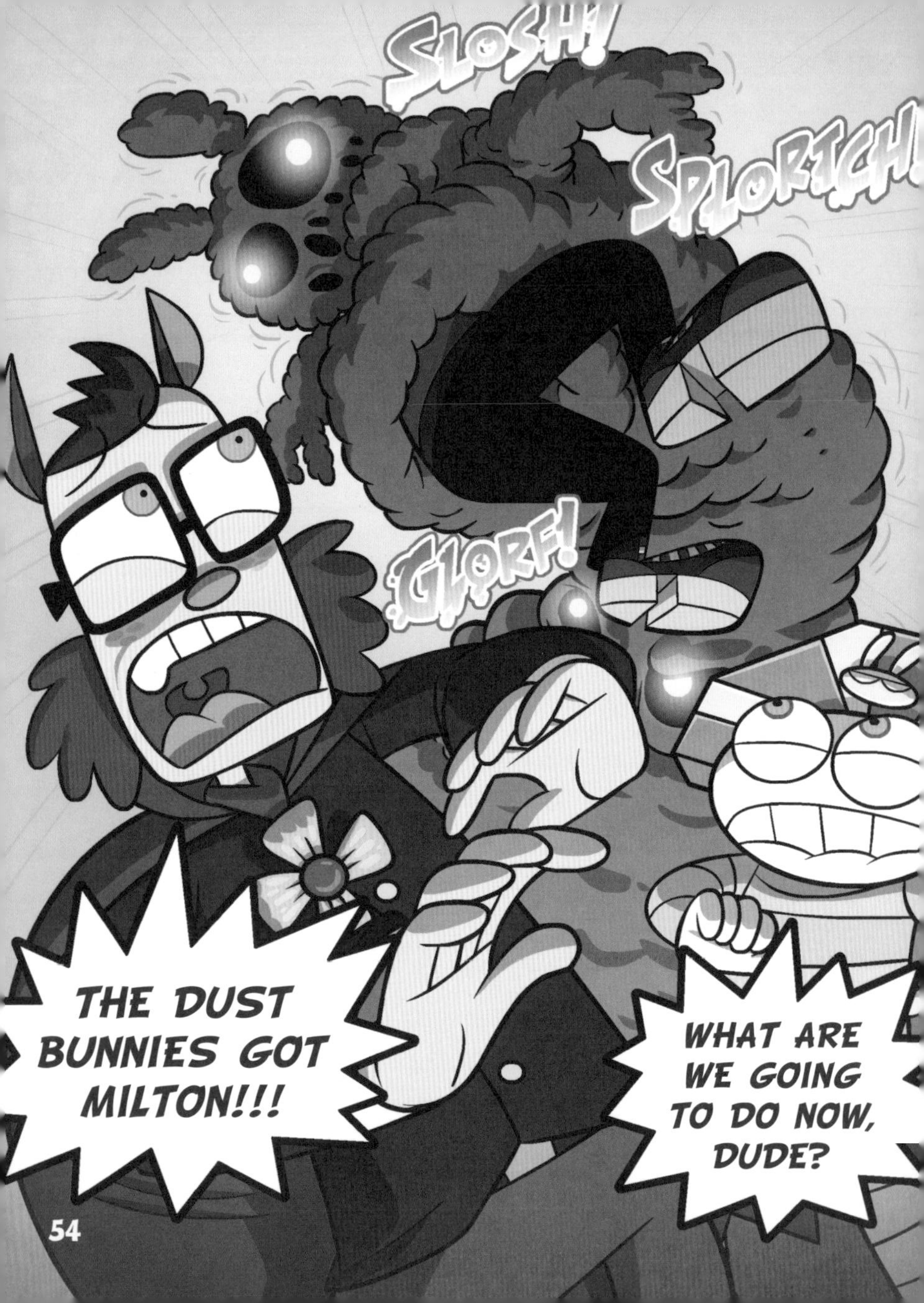
SLOSH!
SPLORTCH!
GLORF!
THE DUST BUNNIES GOT MILTON!!!
WHAT ARE WE GOING TO DO NOW, DUDE?

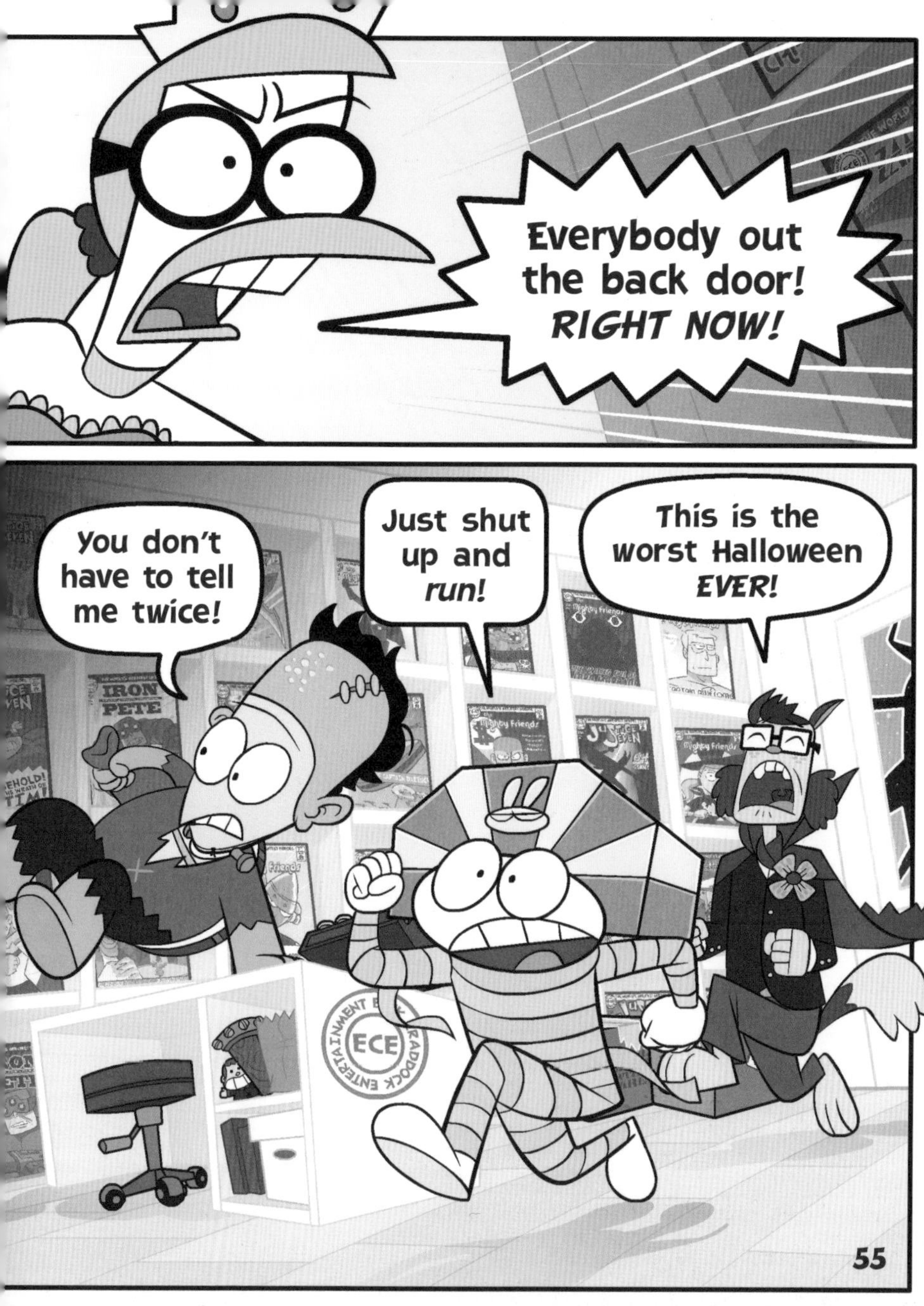
Everybody out the back door! *RIGHT NOW!*
You don't have to tell me twice!
Just shut up and *run!*
This is the worst Halloween *EVER!*

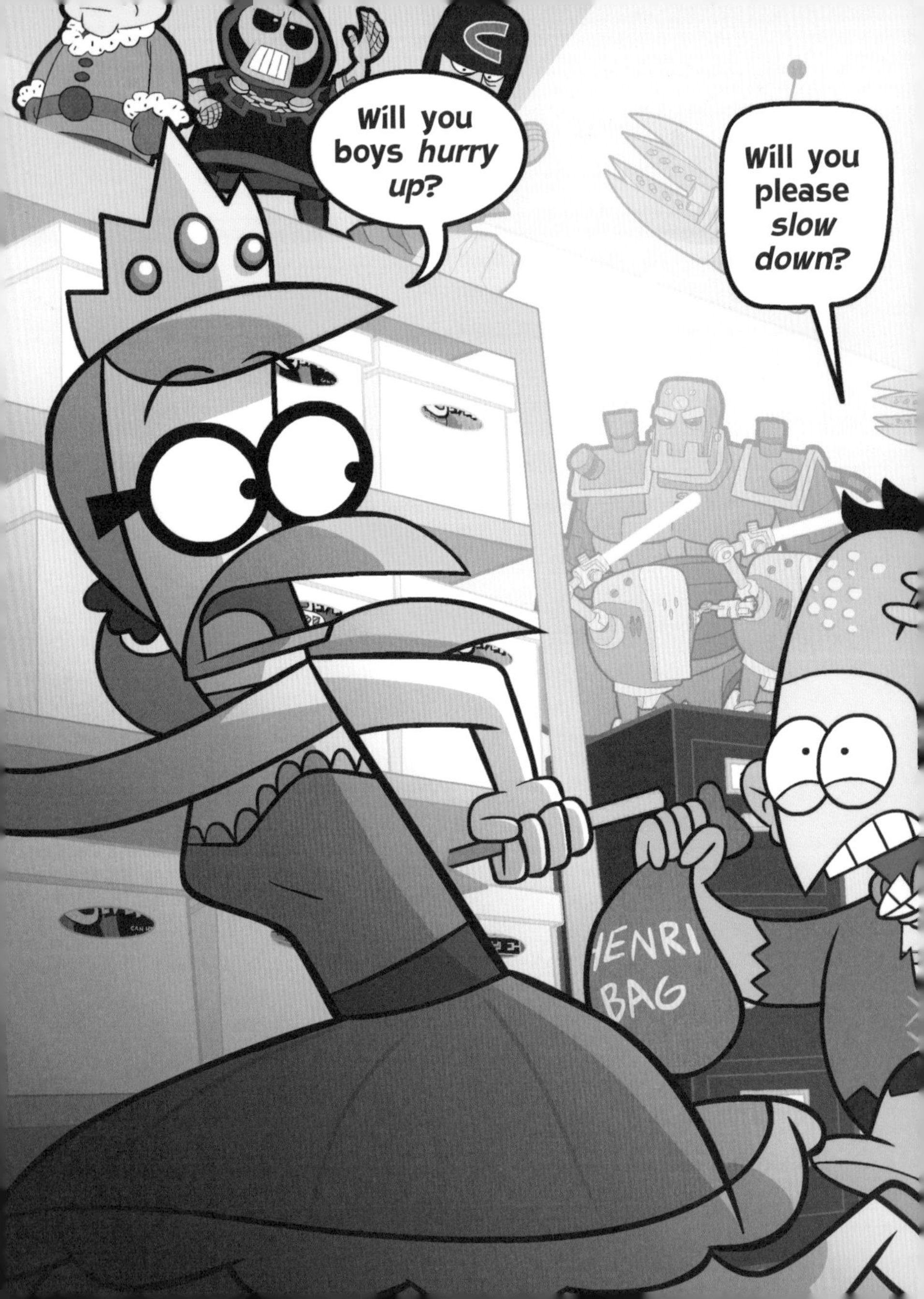
Will you boys hurry up?
Will you please slow down?
HENRI BAG

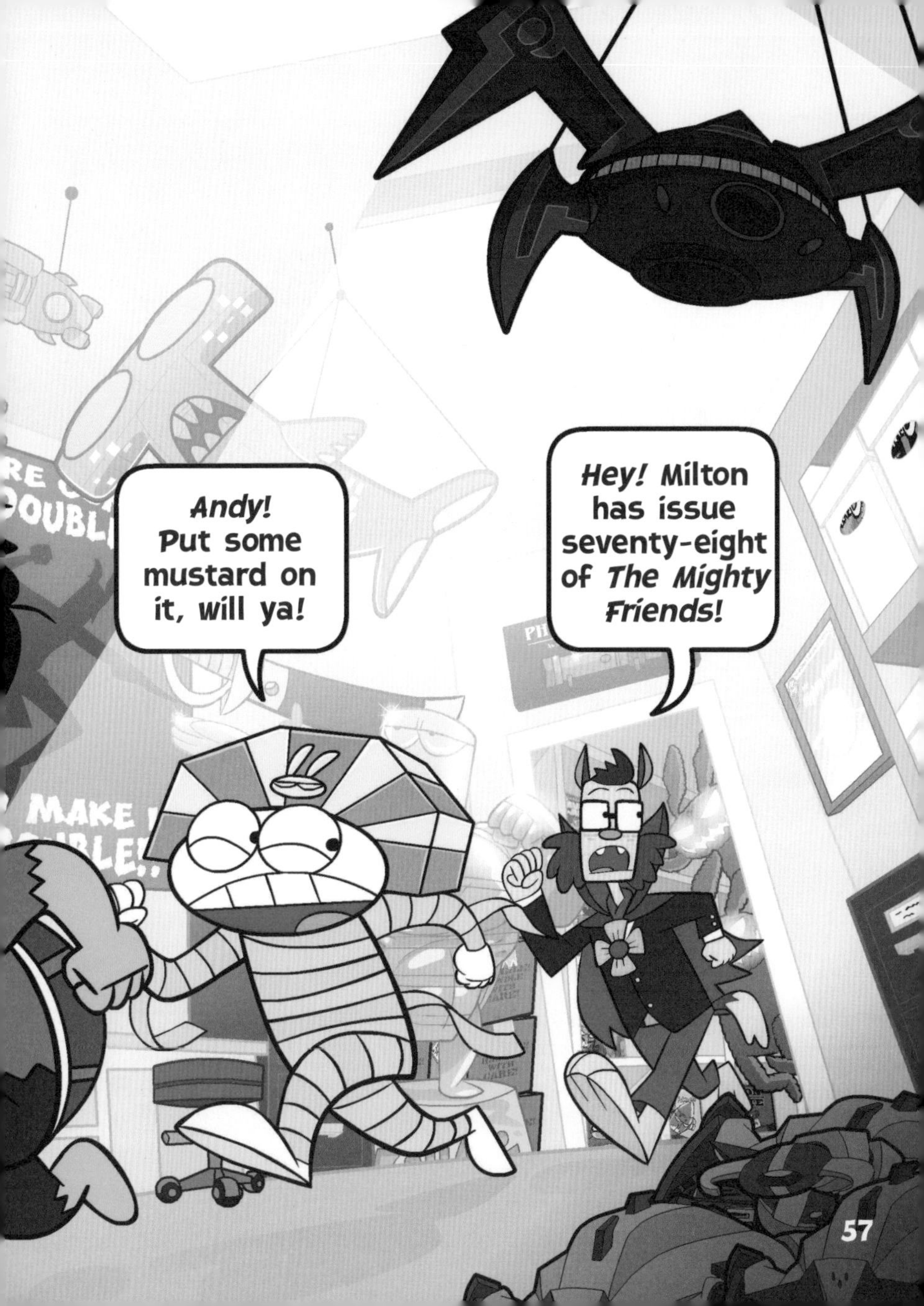

Andy! Put some mustard on it, will ya!
Hey! Milton has issue seventy-eight of *The Mighty Friends!*

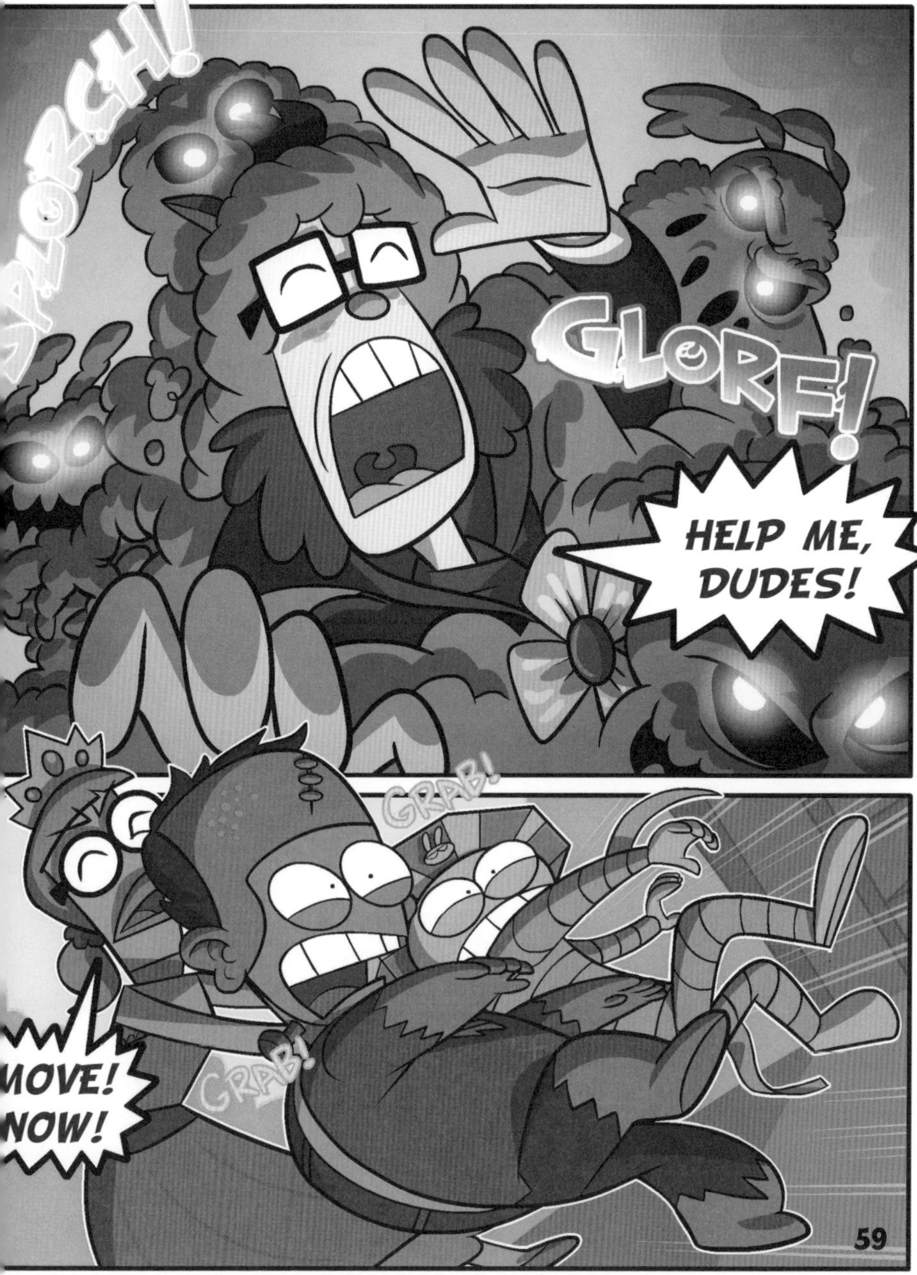
SPLORCH!
GLORF!
HELP ME, DUDES!
GRAB!
MOVE! NOW!
GRAB!

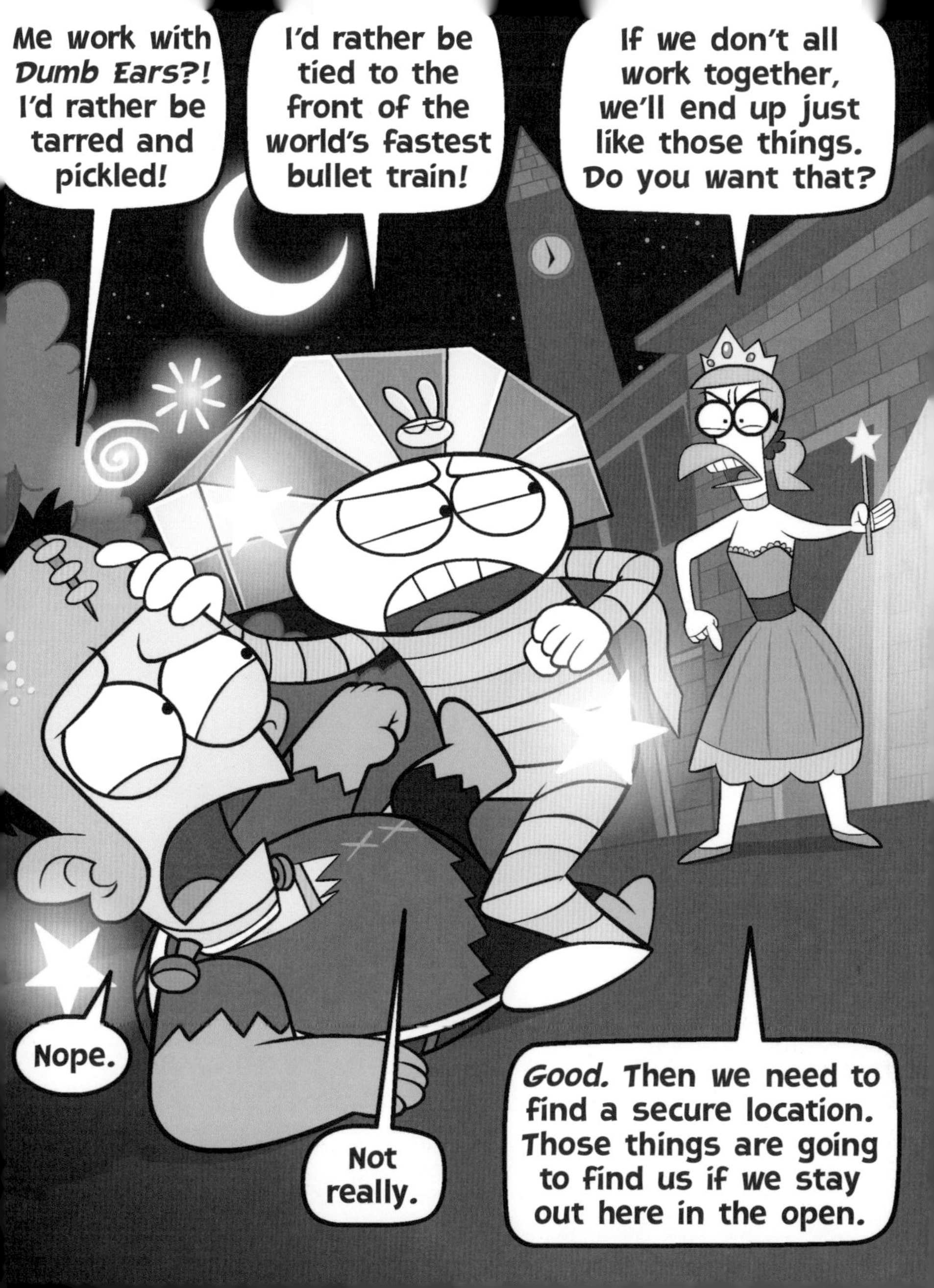
Me work with *Dumb Ears?!* I'd rather be tarred and pickled!
I'd rather be tied to the front of the world's fastest bullet train!
If we don't all work together, we'll end up just like those things. Do you want that?
Nope.
Not really.
Good. Then we need to find a secure location. Those things are going to find us if we stay out here in the open.

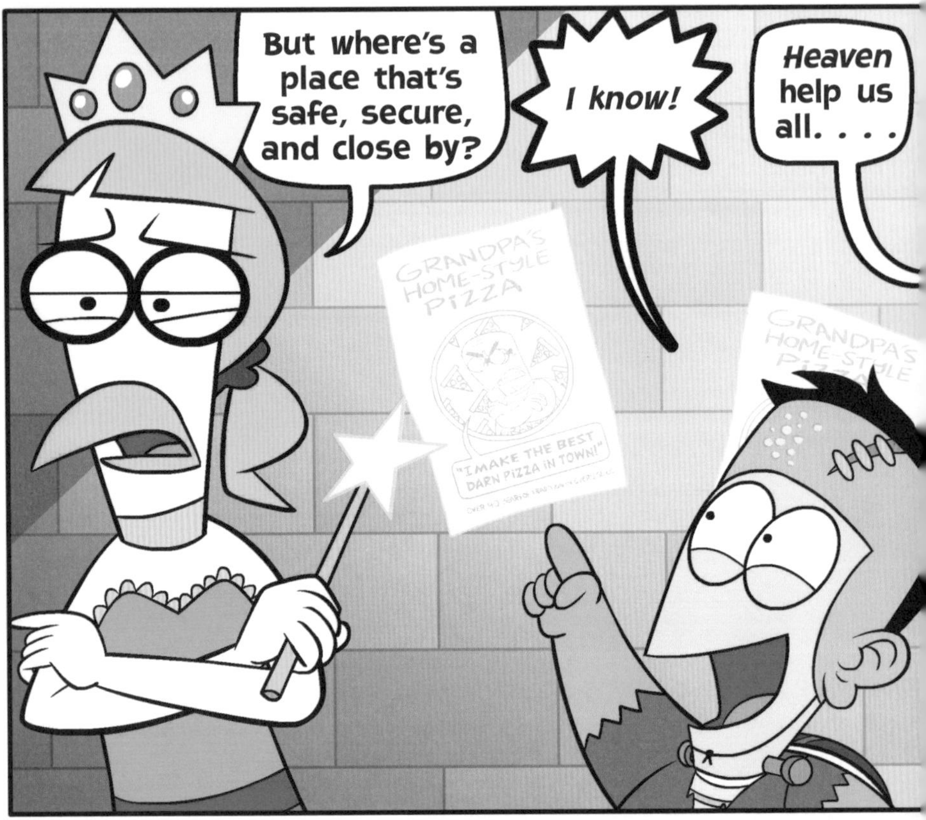
But where's a place that's safe, secure, and close by?
I know!
Heaven help us all. . . .
GRANDPA'S HOME-STYLE PIZZA
"I MAKE THE BEST DARN PIZZA IN TOWN!"
GRANDPA'S HOME-STYLE

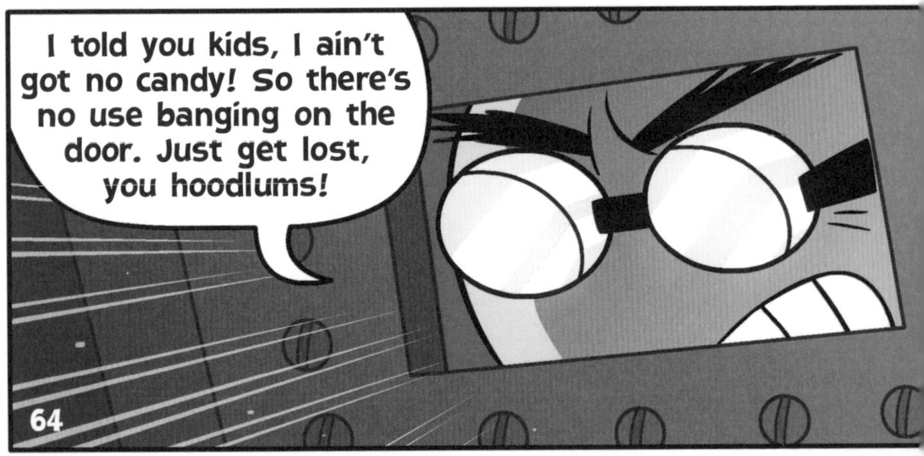
I told you kids, I ain't got no candy! So there's no use banging on the door. Just get lost, you hoodlums!

65

66

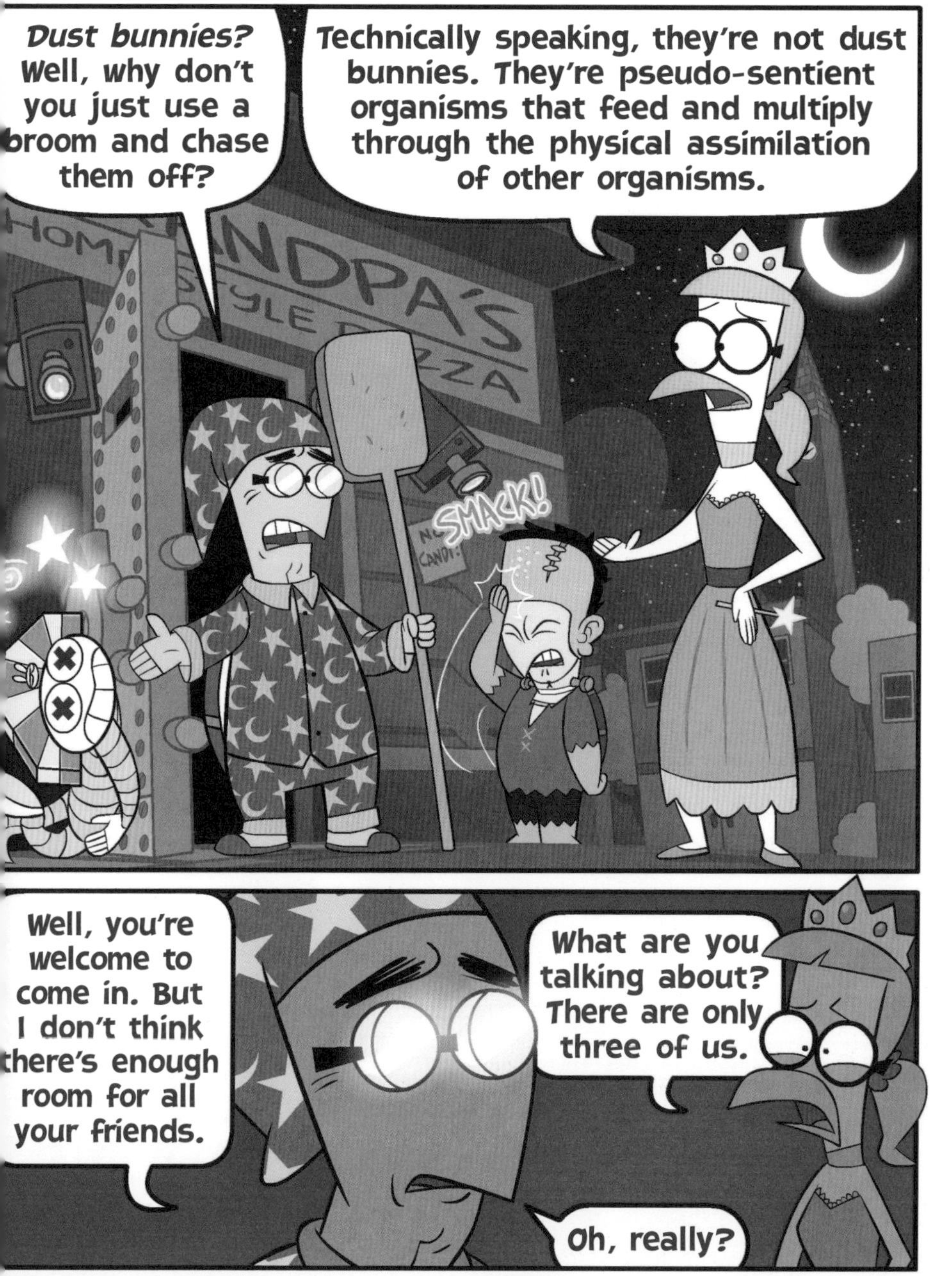
Dust bunnies? Well, why don't you just use a broom and chase them off?
Technically speaking, they're not dust bunnies. They're pseudo-sentient organisms that feed and multiply through the physical assimilation of other organisms.
SMACK!
Well, you're welcome to come in. But I don't think there's enough room for all your friends.
What are you talking about? There are only three of us.
Oh, really?

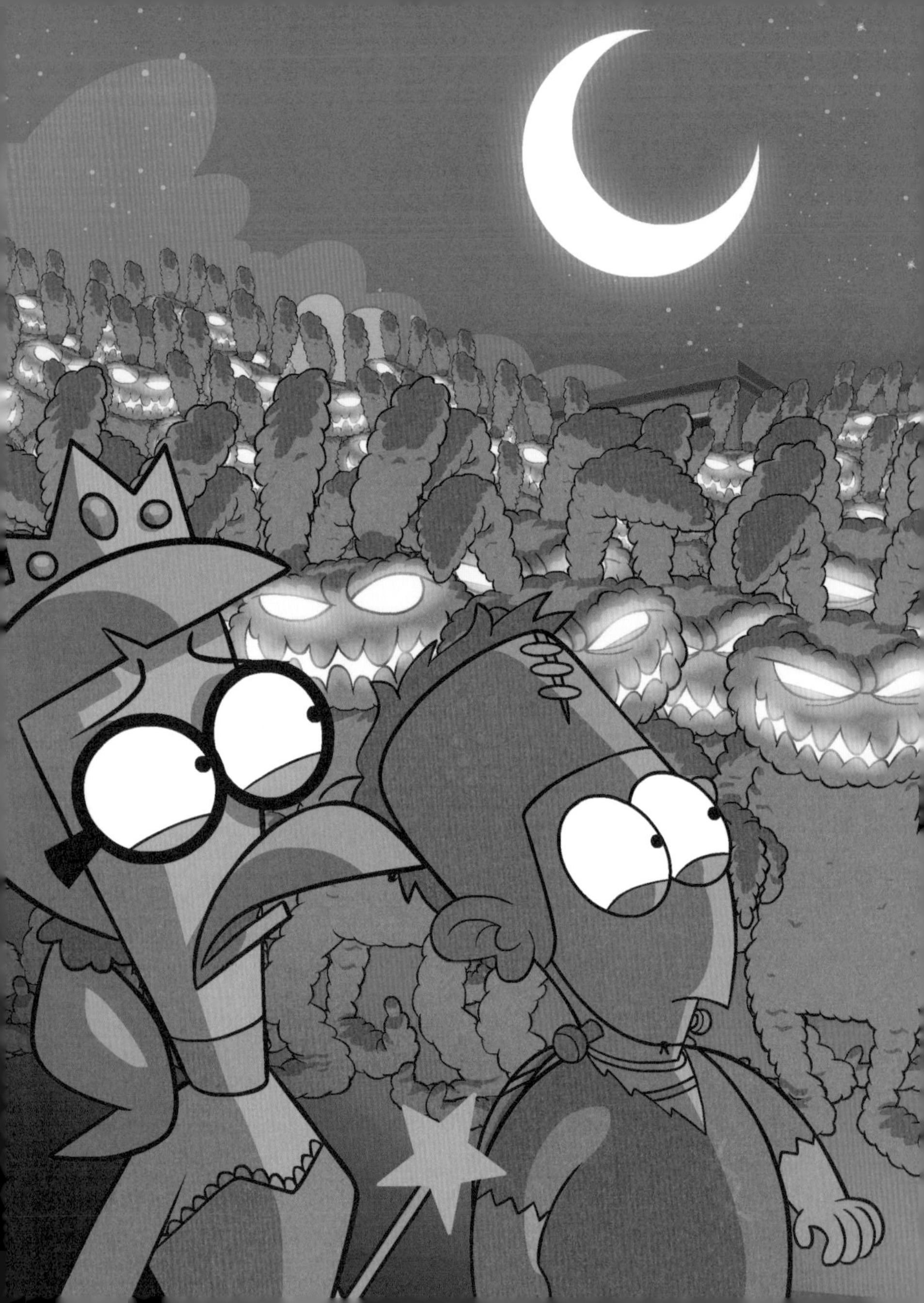

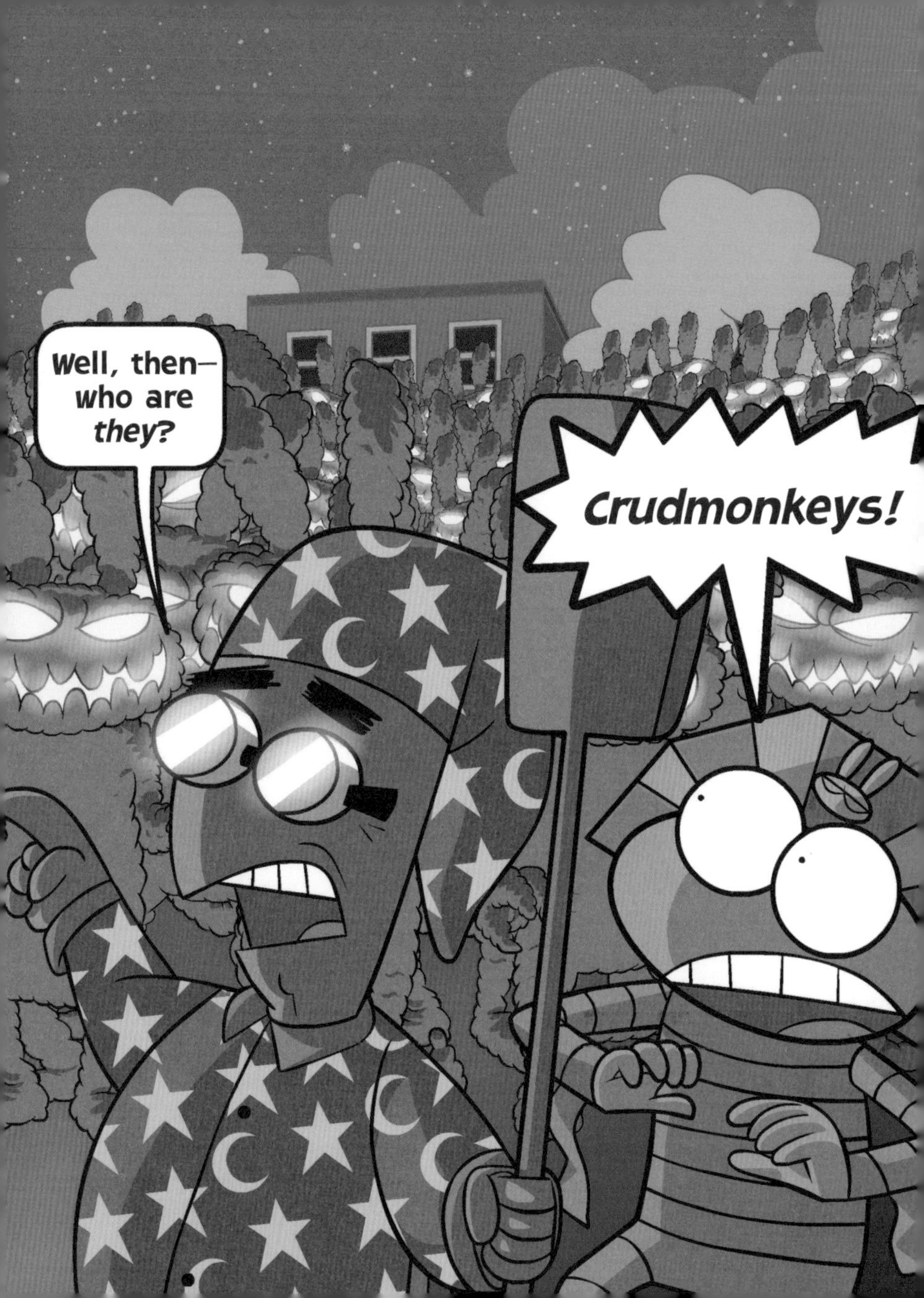
Well, then—
who are
they?
Crudmonkeys!

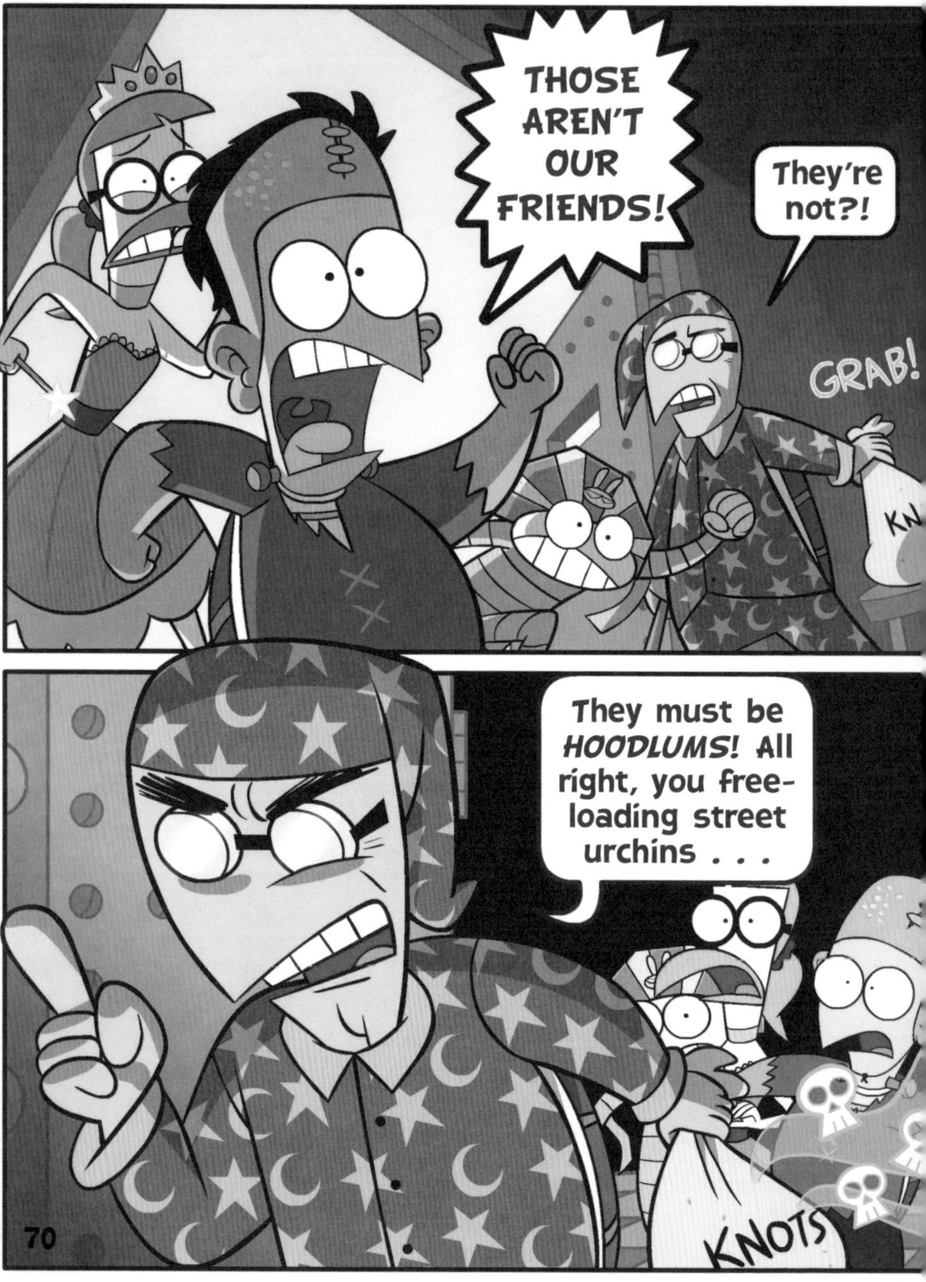
THOSE AREN'T OUR FRIENDS!
They're not?!
GRAB!
They must be *HOODLUMS!* All right, you free-loading street urchins . . .
KNOTS

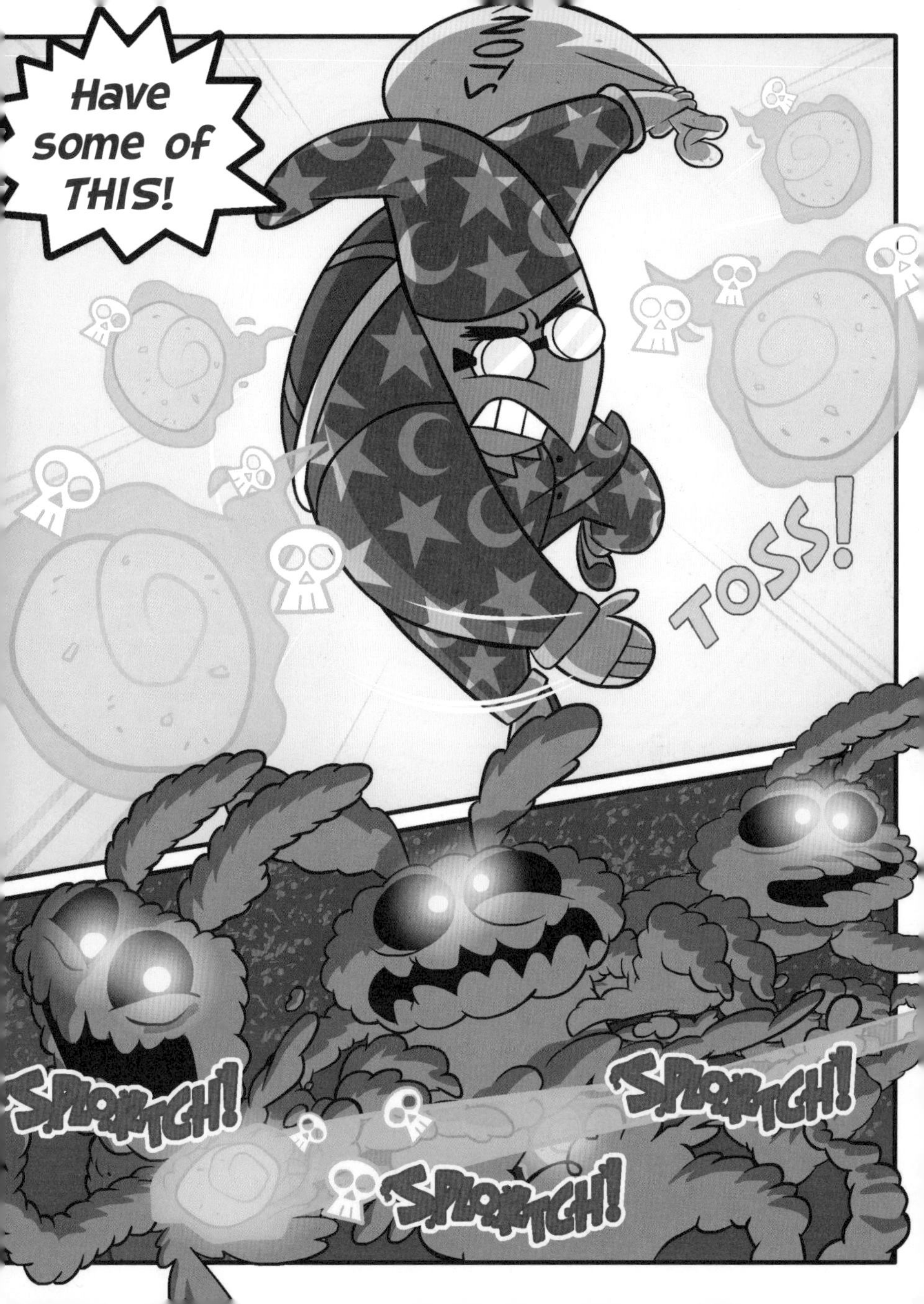
Have some of THIS!
SNOT
TOSS!
SPLORTCH!
SPLORTCH!
SPLORTCH!

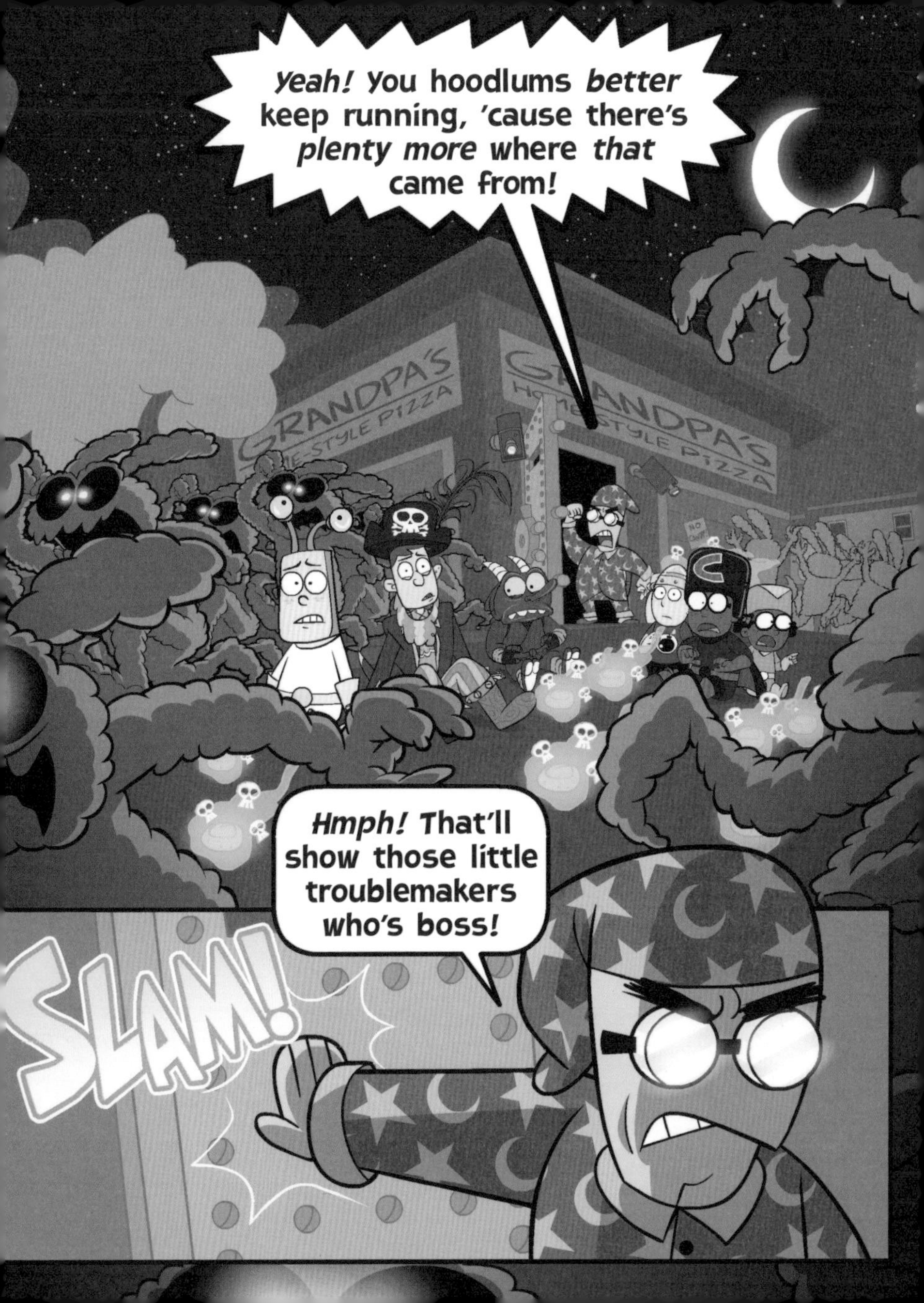
Yeah! You hoodlums better keep running, 'cause there's plenty more where that came from!
GRANDPA'S HOME-STYLE PIZZA
GRANDPA'S HOME-STYLE PIZZA
Hmph! That'll show those little troublemakers who's boss!
SLAM!

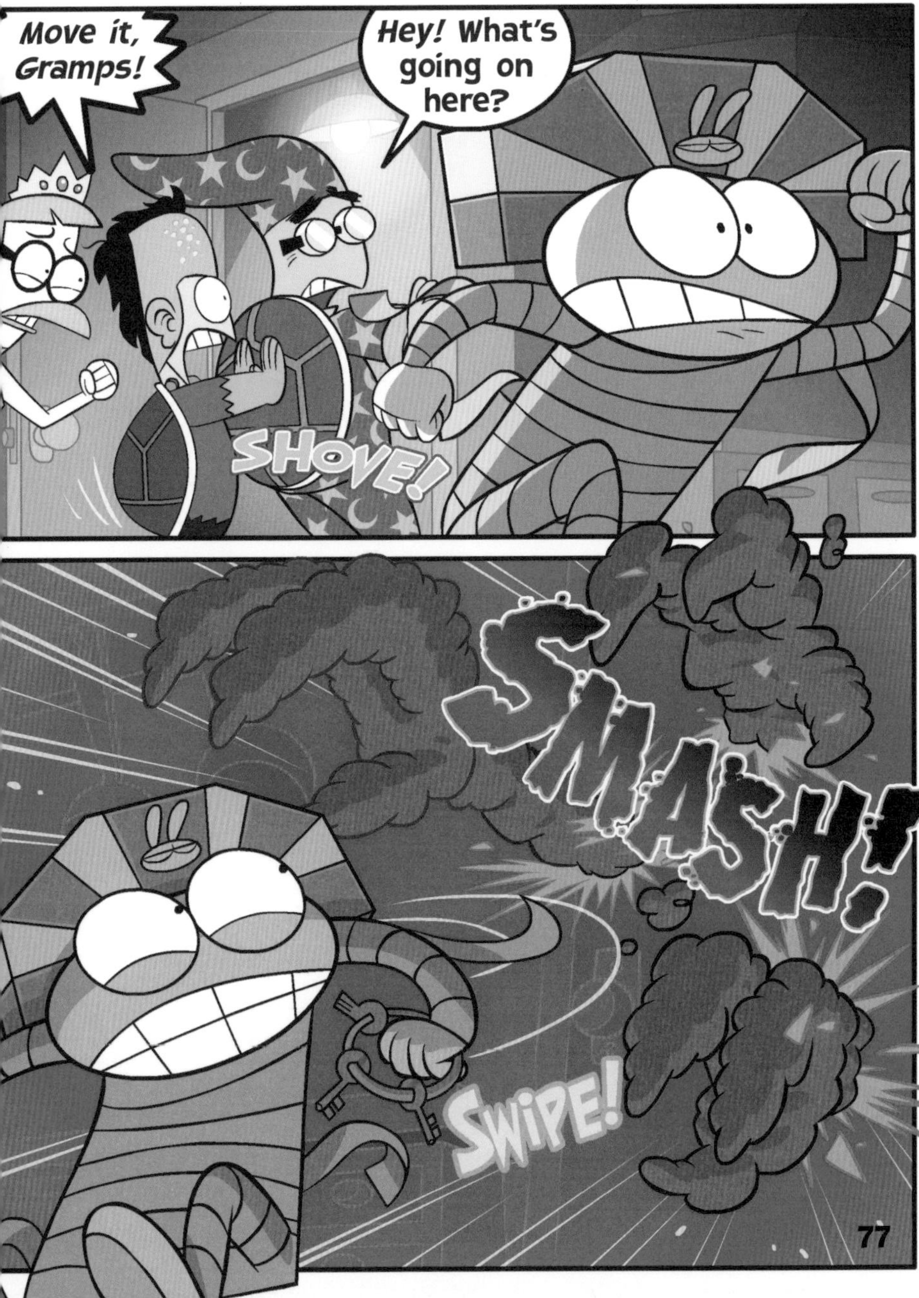
Move it, Gramps!
Hey! What's going on here?
SHOVE!
SMASH!
SWIPE!

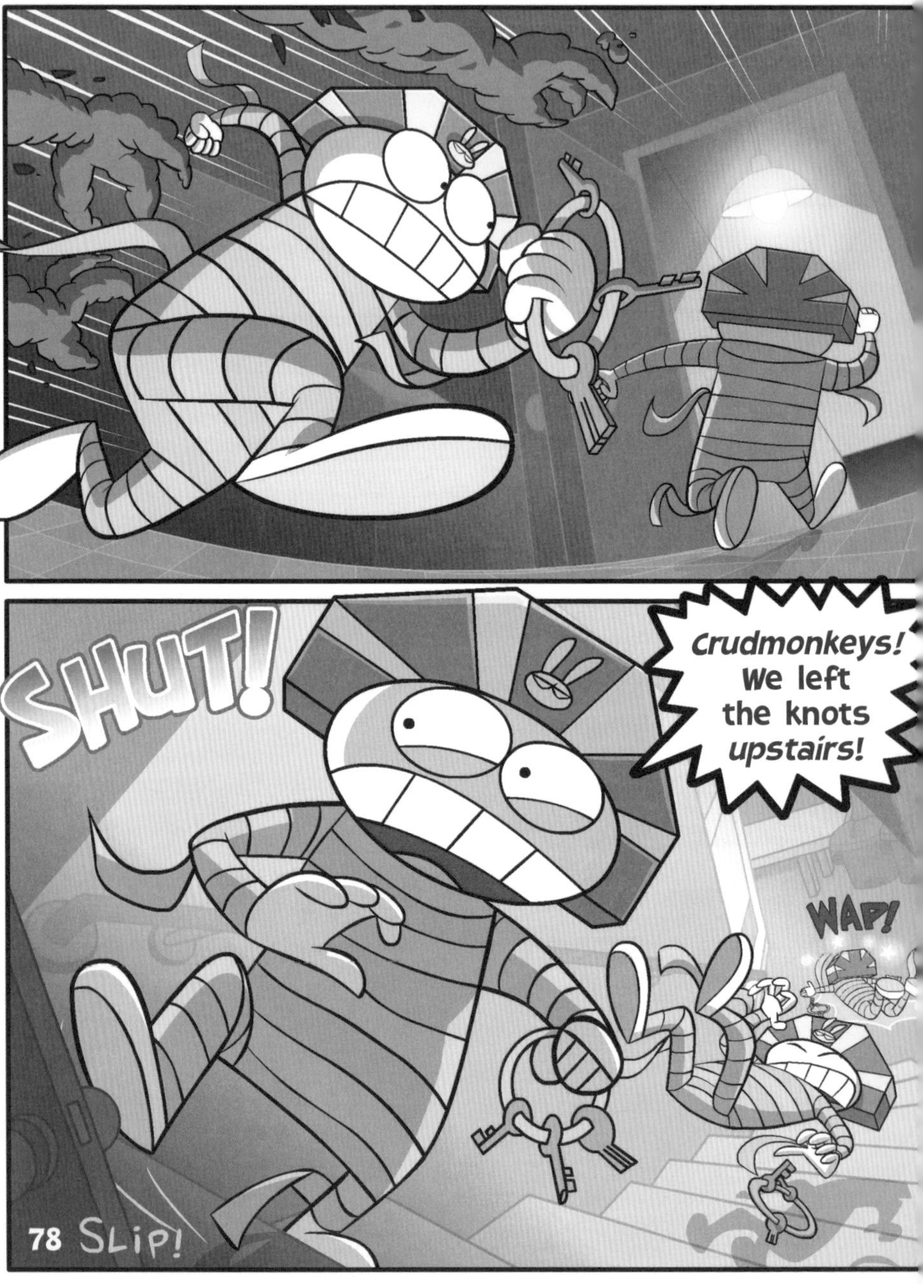
SHUT!
Crudmonkeys! We left the knots upstairs!
WAP!
SLIP!

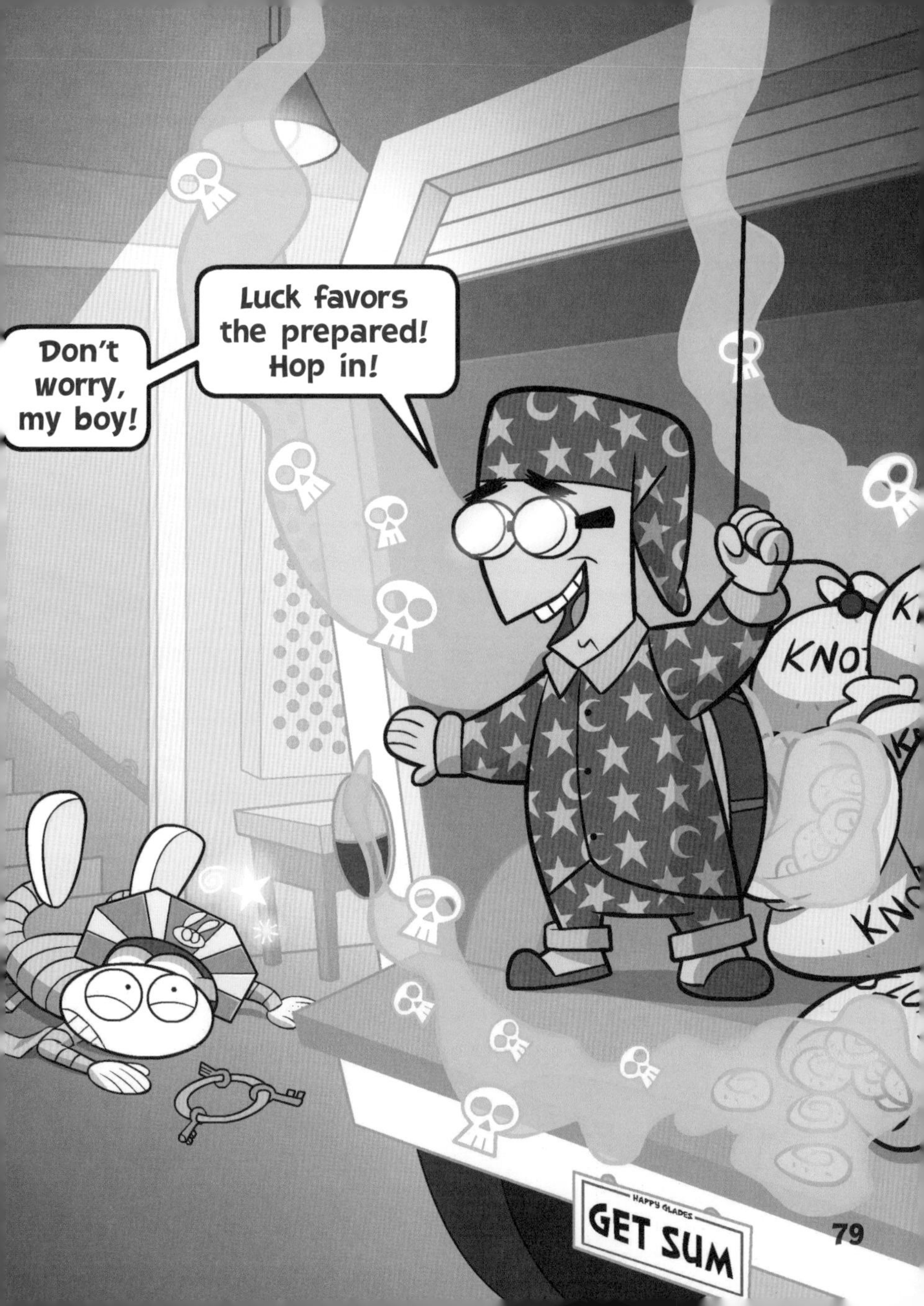
Don't worry, my boy!
Luck favors the prepared! Hop in!
KNOT
HAPPY GLADES
GET SUM

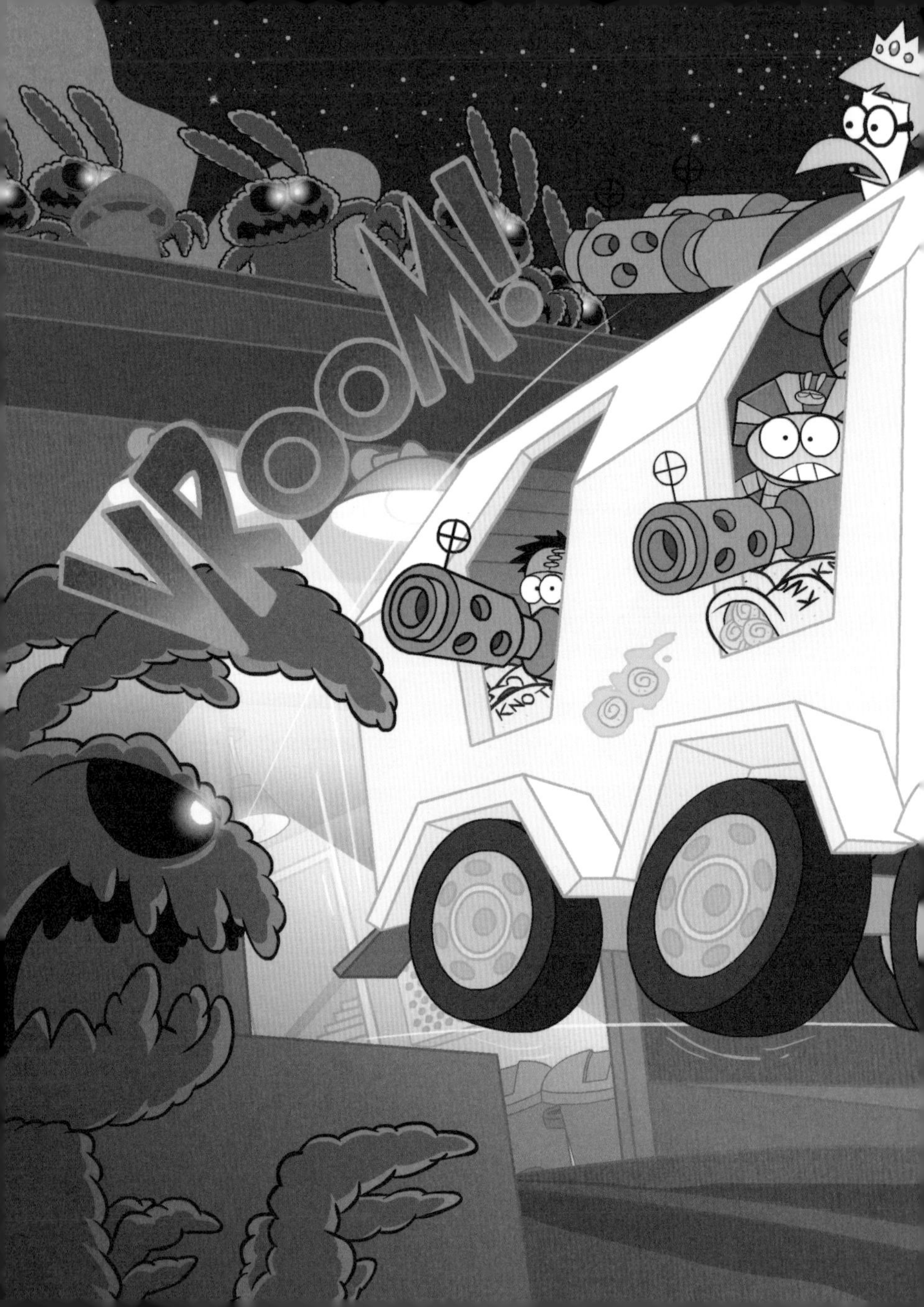
VROOM!
KNOT

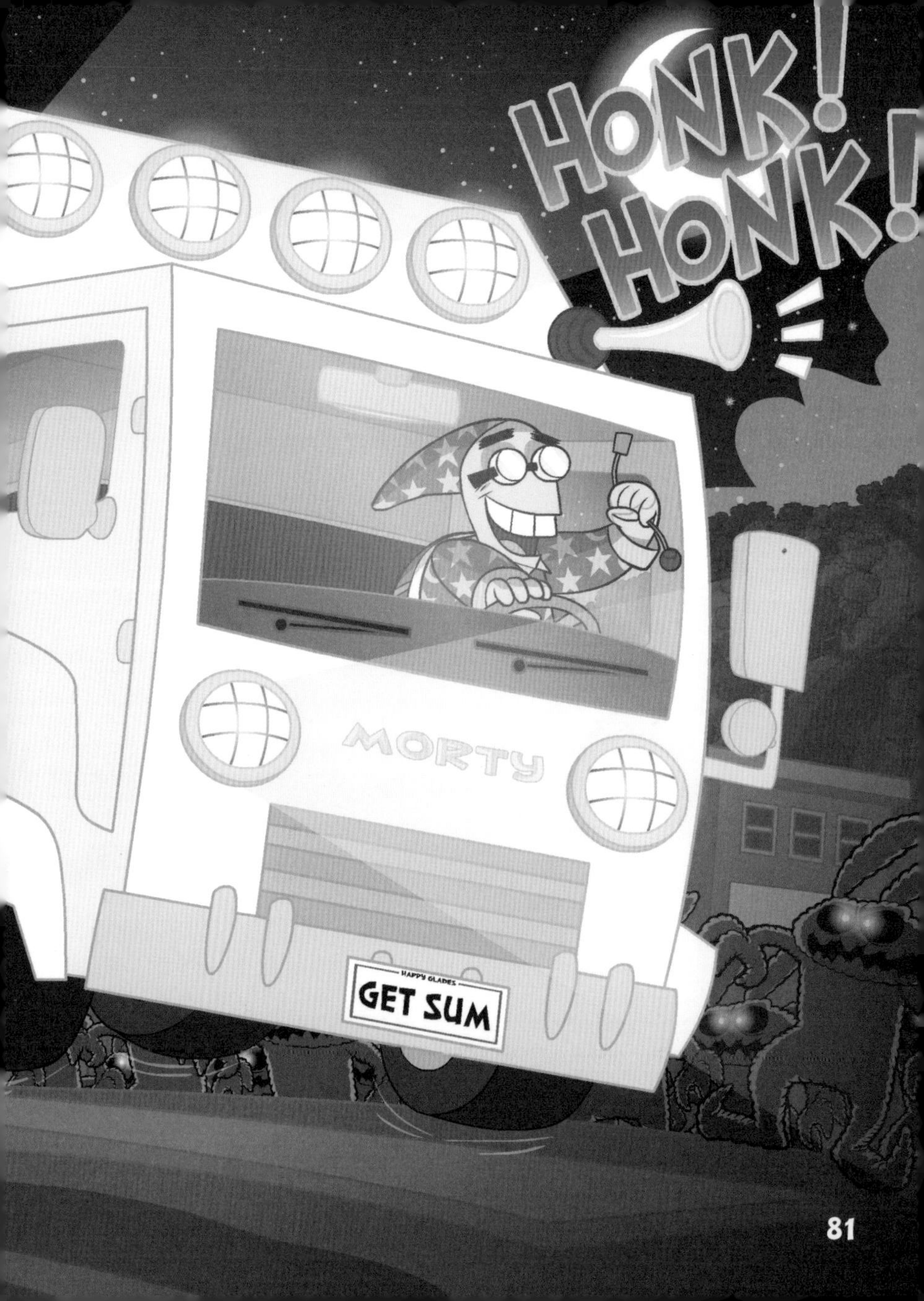
HONK! HONK!
MORTY
HAPPY GLADES
GET SUM

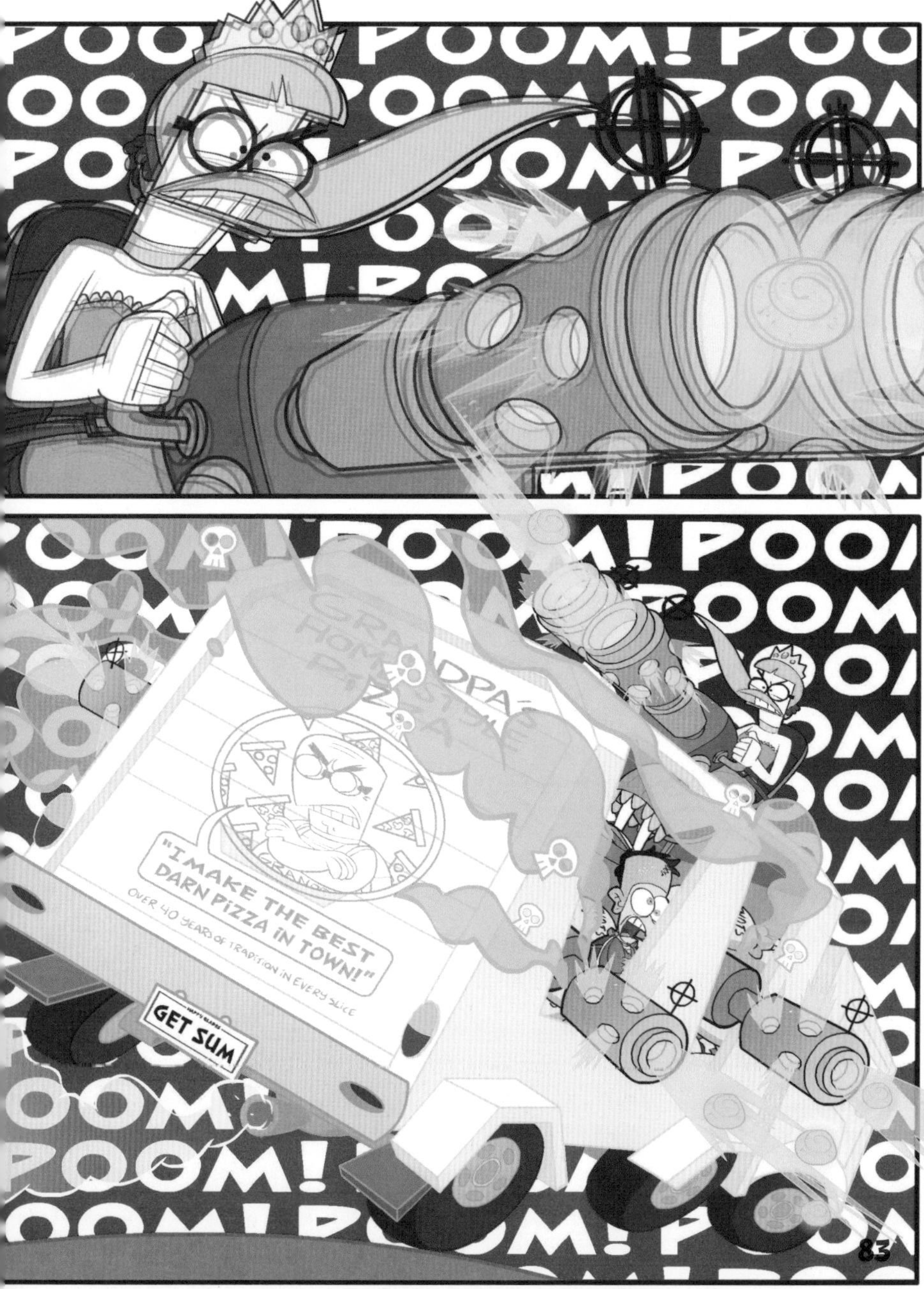
POOM! POOM! POOM!
"I MAKE THE BEST DARN PIZZA IN TOWN!"
OVER 40 YEARS OF TRADITION IN EVERY SLICE
GET SUM

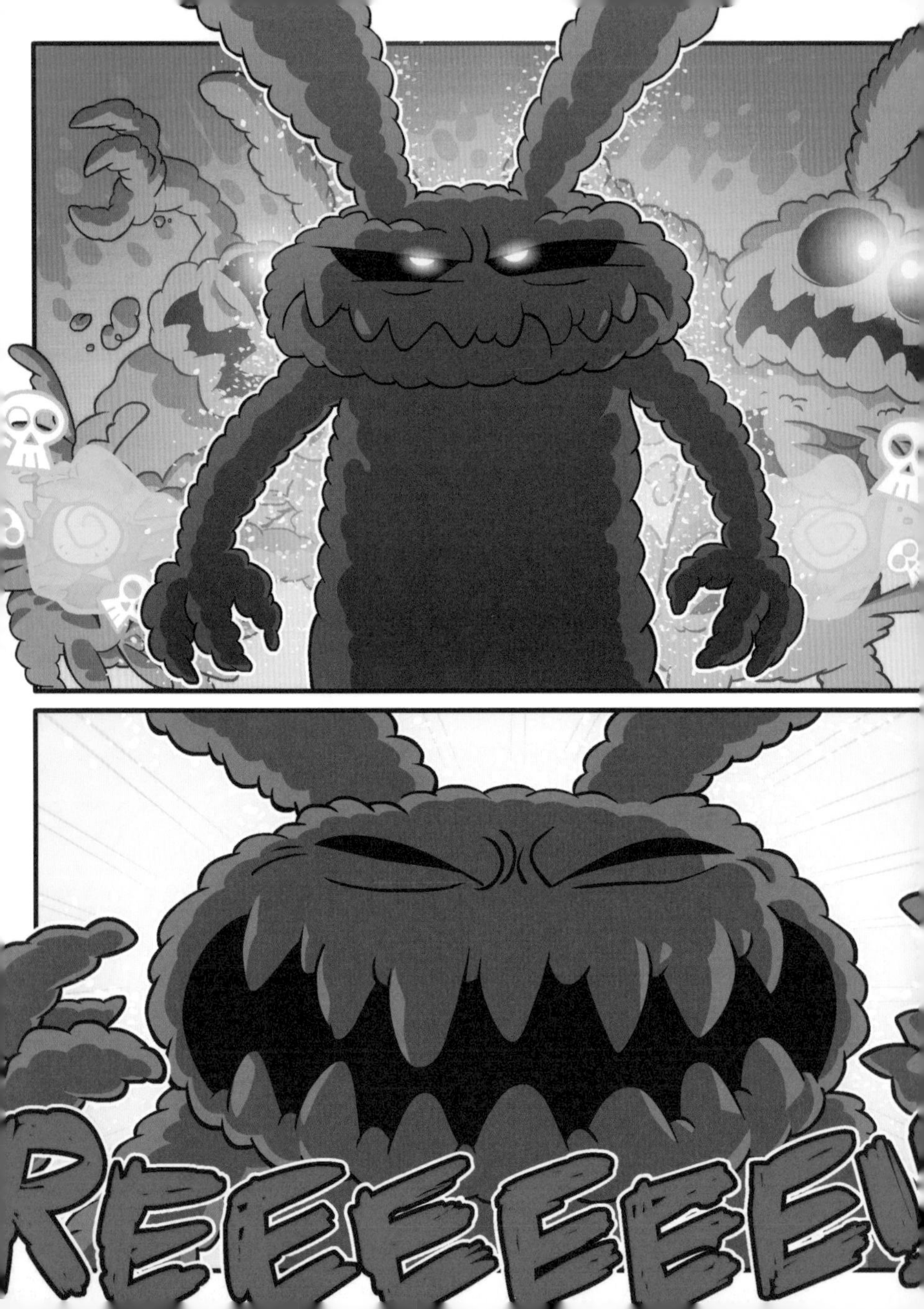
REEEEEE!

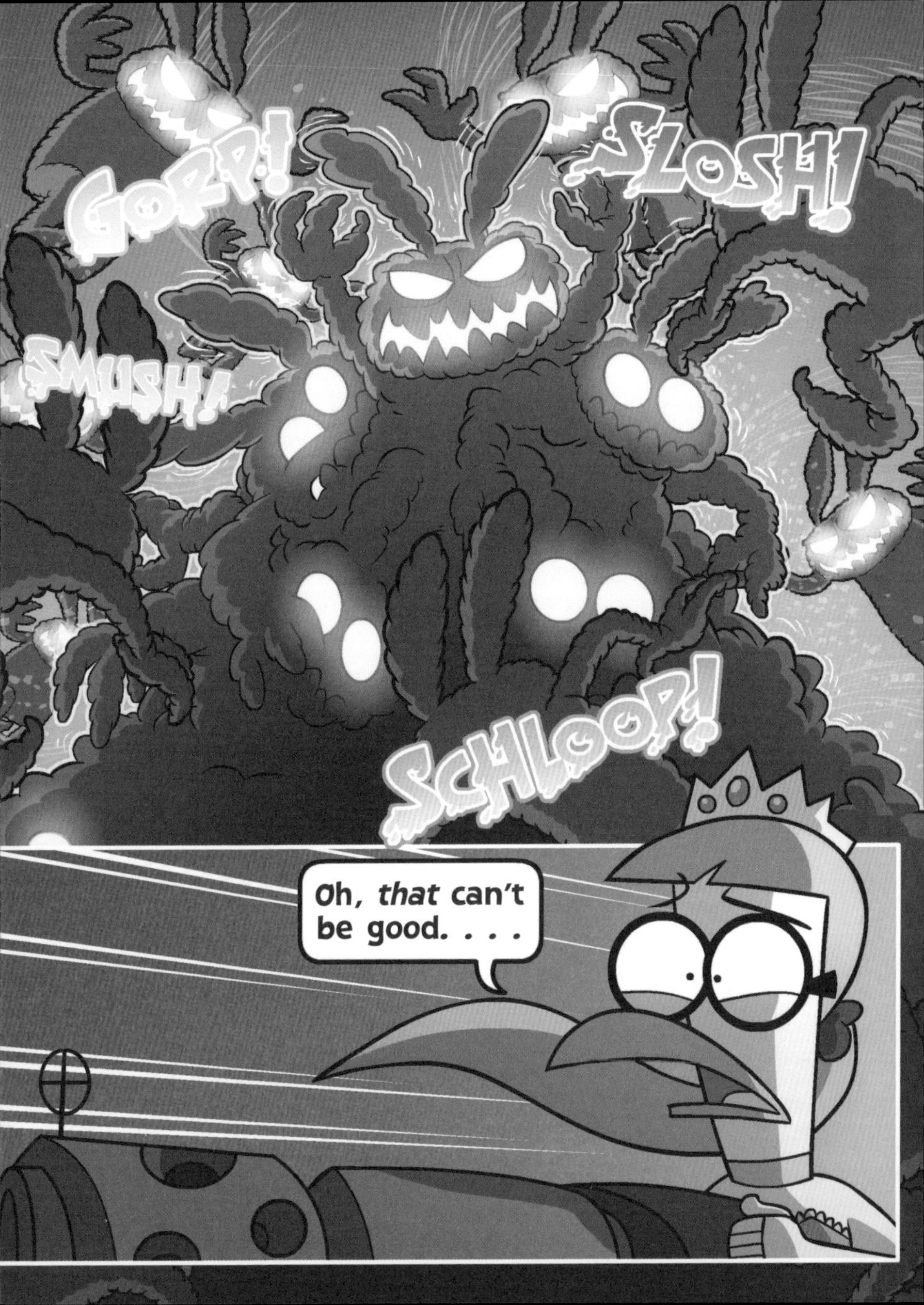
GORP!
SLOSH!
SMUSH!
SCHLOOP!
Oh, *that* can't be good. . . .

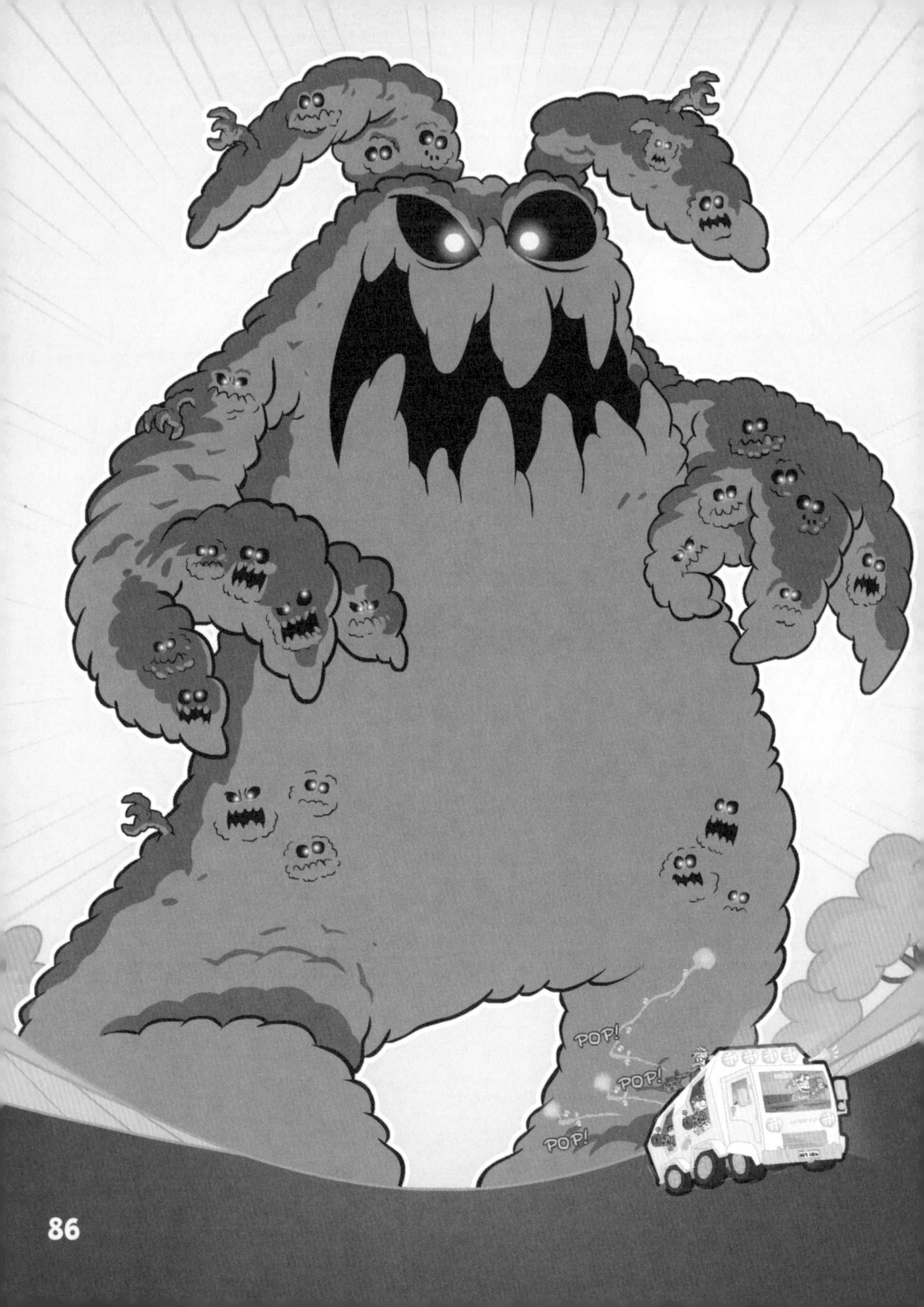
POP!
POP!
POP!

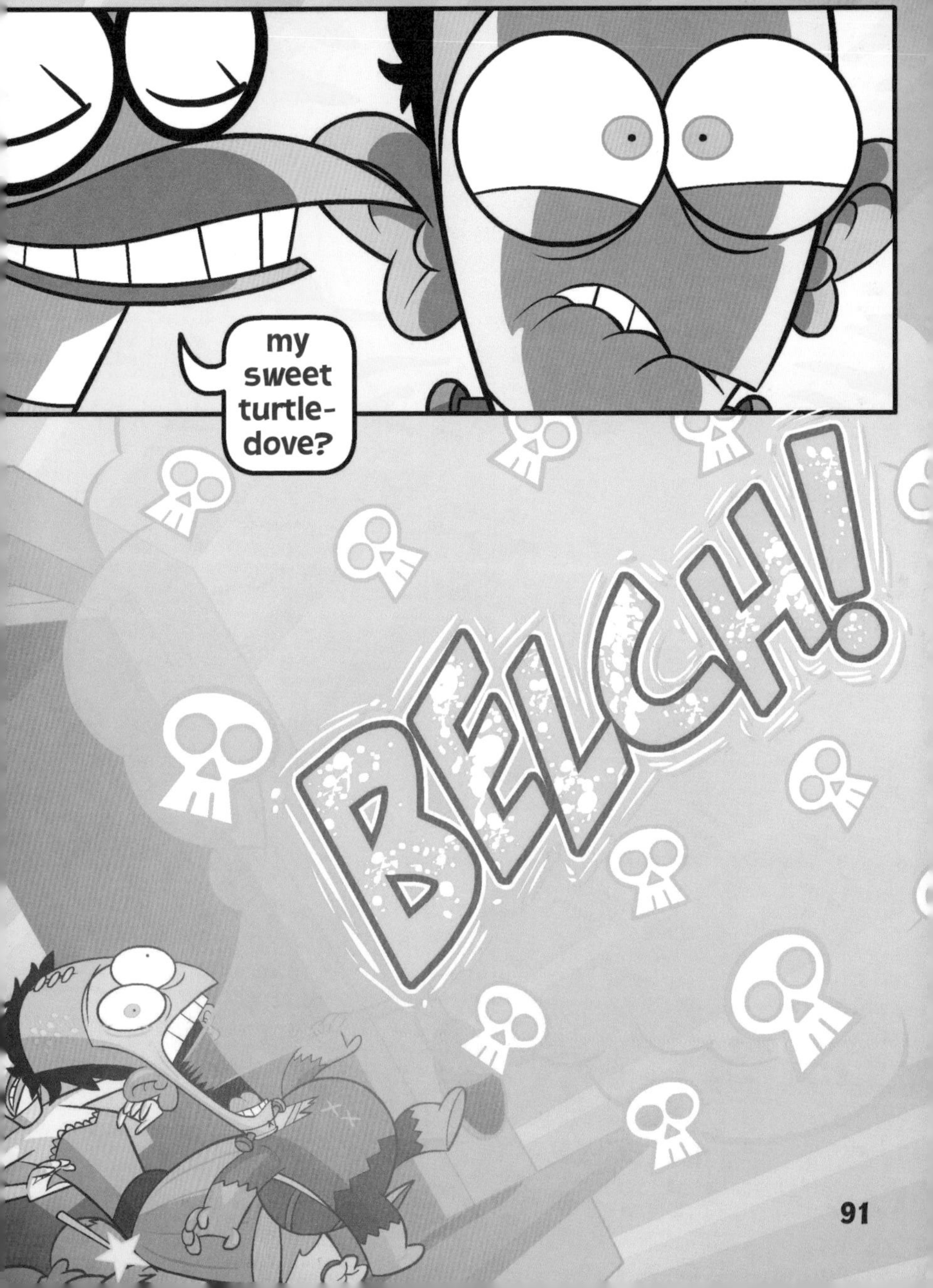
my sweet turtle-dove?
BELCH!

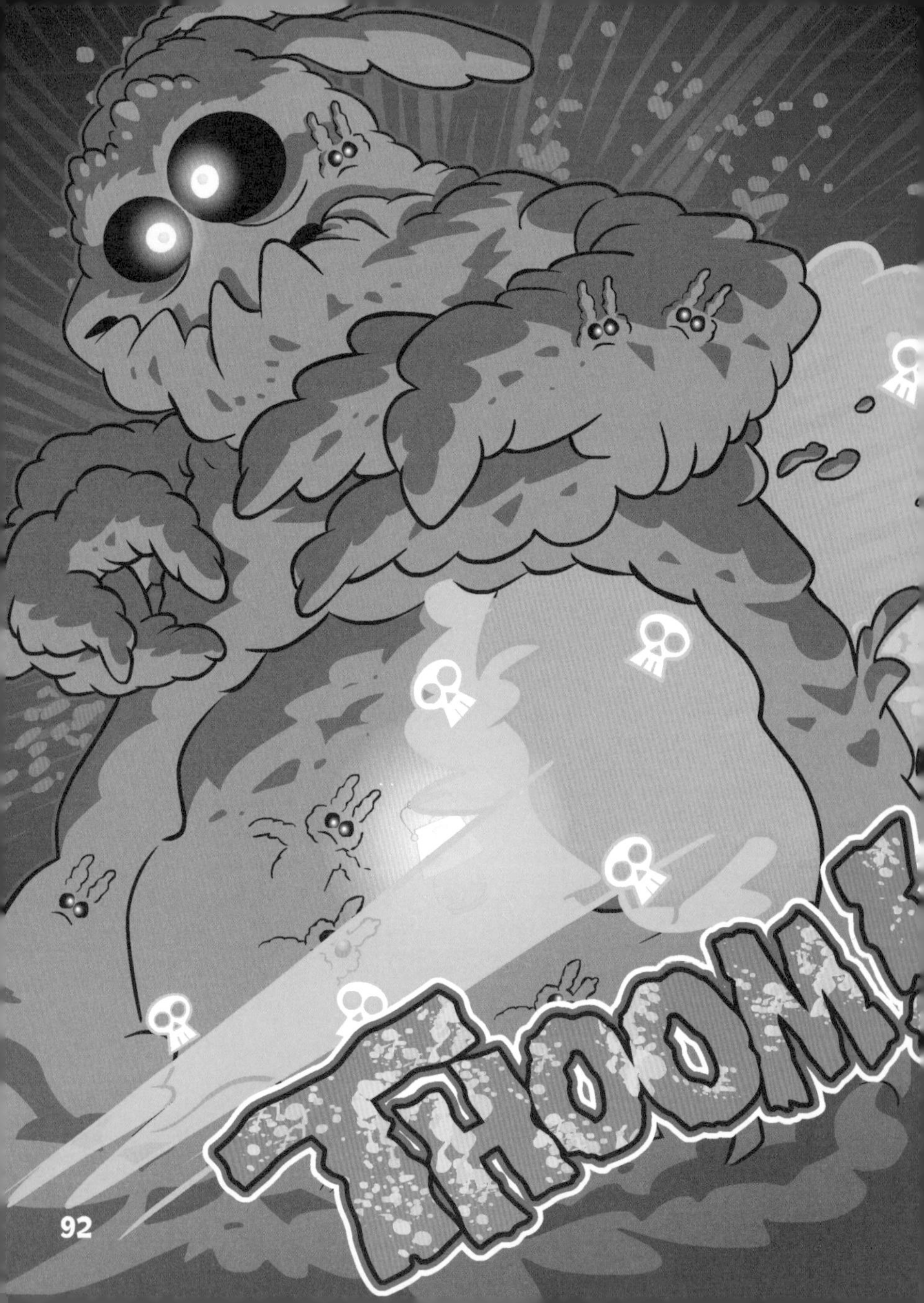
THOOM!

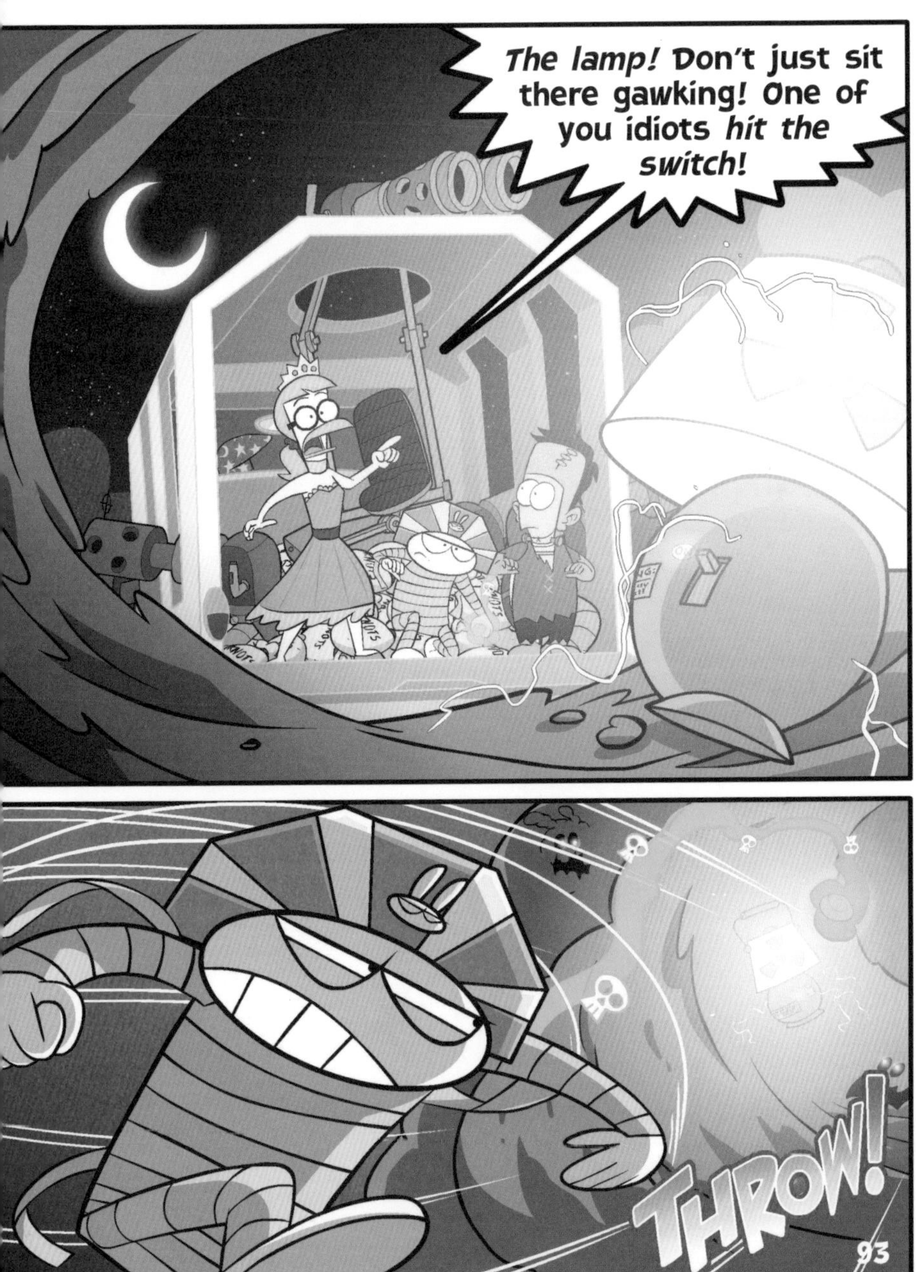
The lamp! Don't just sit there gawking! One of you idiots *hit the switch!*
THROW!

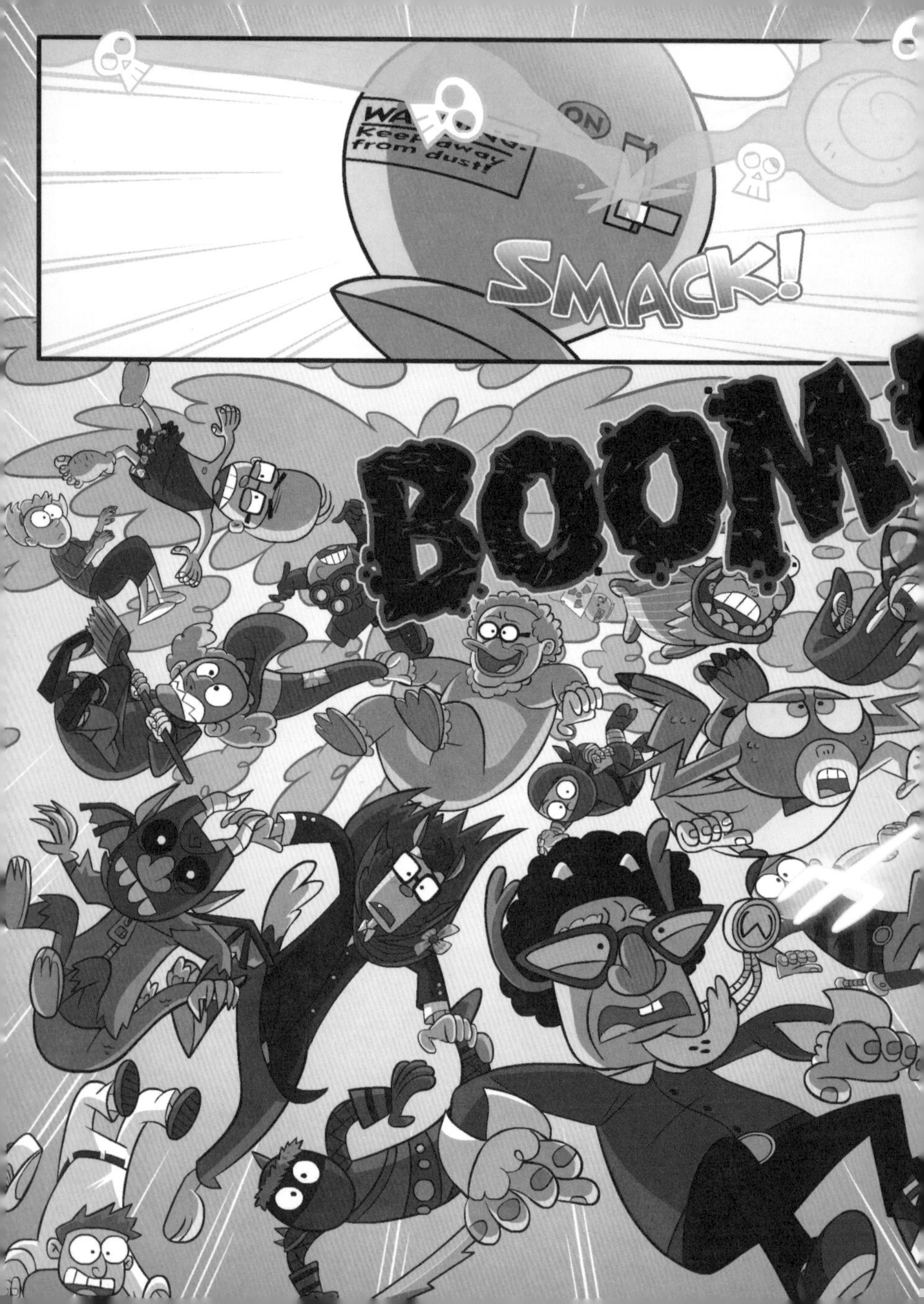

Keep away from dust!
ON
SMACK!
BOOM